BLOOD VENGEANCE

Tanner McKitrick rode his gray bronc upstreet toward the speaker's platform in front of the Claremont Hotel and the man he was about to kill. Snugged under his somber black coat was a Navy Colt, the tip of the worn leather holster barely showing. It had been agreed after some heated debate with his brother Wade that Tanner would have the more dangerous job of pressing into the crowd and coming in at the speaker's platform from the front. He knew that Wade would rely on his Henry as he shared in the killing of the senator from Montana, Johnston Pettigrew.

With a pleasant smile plucking his lips, Tanner edged his horse through the crowd listening to the speech of the man who'd doublecrossed them back in Montana. What Tanner wanted now was for Pettigrew to lock glances, to know the McKitricks had caught up with him.

"So again I tell you we must protect our freedoms . . ." Johnston Pettigrew's voice faltered as his eyes spanned across the street at Tanner McKitrick. A wild gleam of fear and disbelief came into his eyes.

"Vengeance is ours!" cried out Tanner McKitrick as he doffed his hat and reached for his holstered revolver. . . .

ROBERT KAMMEN
KILLING DAY AT SQUAW GAP

ZEBRA BOOKS
KENSINGTON PUBLISHING CORP.

ZEBRA BOOKS

are published by

Kensington Publishing Corp.
475 Park Avenue South
New York, NY 10016

First printing: July, 1990

Printed in the United States of America

FOR KATHLEEN OF THE CLAN ROBINSON—
who has weathered many a storm with a smile or
a kind word . . .

Chapter One

A tiger salamander wiggled onto a rail still humming from the passing of a Union Pacific freight train. The yellow and black striped skin of the salamander shone dully under a noon sun as it lifted its head and took in the strange sight a few rods away, of workmen driving steel spikes into wooden crossties, prison guards brandishing rifles and soldiers idling by a locomotive spewing out smoke. Just this morning its burrow had been torn apart by men yielding pickaxes, and being a creature of the night, the salamander found itself in an alien world. Now it felt alarming vibrations in the form of boots rasping against the stony ground, and with the tiger salamander hissing out its long tongue, it spun around.

"Got'cha!" exulted one of the prison guards as his unleashed bullwhip snapped out at the salamander, to have it wiggle spasmodically before dying. "Got'cha, you devilish critter." Loutish eyes smiled out of the face of guard Damon Schwartz, then curling up his bullwhip, he bent over and grasped the salamander by the tail.

"That was nice work, Damon, but wat'cha gonna do with that thing?"

"This is gonna make a nice dinner for McKitrick."

Hefting his rifle, the other guard chortled as he paced along the railbed after Damon Schwartz.

7

They stepped past the triple-tier passenger cars housing the prisoners and the engine facing to the west along new track being laid.

Farther along the railroad right-of-way, a prisoner named Wade McKitrick sighed wearily when the whistle sounded to tell them it was the noon hour. His workworn and lacerated hands were wrapped around the handle of a sledgehammer, but until three months ago all they'd known was the feel of gun metal. Like the other prisoners sent out here from the territorial prison at Laramie, Wade McKitrick wore leg irons. As had some, he'd shucked the cotton shirt. Sweat beaded his face and stung into his eyes. He was around five eleven, leaned out and holding back his anger. It was because of his reputation that he'd been singled out for special attention. More often than not when hammering another spike into a crosstie there'd be a crackling hiss followed by the leather thongs of a bullwhip snaking around his naked torso, cutting into flesh and sometimes to buckle his knees. He'd stomached enough of this hellacious work gang and that bullwhip of Damon Schwartz's.

"Would the breakout happen today?"

The words passed through Wade McKitrick's parched lips as he stared around at the harsh and forbidding prairie stretching toward the blue-dimmed horizon. At the moment they were laying track at a place called Point of Rocks, with appropriately named Bitter Creek just to the east, the humps of varying mountain ranges quartering around them. Closer, he took in the jumbled pile of rocks littering rugged elevations, and the draws working in toward the right-of-way. And the twenty

8

or so soldiers here to supposedly guard them from marauding Indians. The prisoners were kept isolated from others working here, white men along with a gang of Chinese used mainly to manhandle rocks or set dynamite charges, and with all of these workers being paid a dollar a day plus board. Whereas money earned by the prisoners was to be given them upon their being released from prison.

"A cold day in hell if we see any of that money," spat out Wade McKitrick as he threw the sledgehammer down at a railing.

"Hold it right there, McKitrick! The rest of you scum!"

McKitrick, and some other prisoners, broke stride and swung around to turn sullen eyes upon Damon Schwartz ambling toward them. Three other guards moved a shade closer, to smile when Schwartz called out, "You, McKitrick, look what I done brought for you."

"Now aren't you the helpful sonofabitch."

"That's right, McKitrick, I always told you that smart mouth of yours would get you into trouble."

Then Wade McKitrick gazed down at the dead salamander landing at his feet, and he said tautly, "Schwartz, you can shove that where the sun don't shine."

"Yup, keep jawing away, McKitrick." His jaw working angrily, the guard strode in closer and unleashed a stream of tobacco juice.

Some of the bitter juice and saliva found Wade McKitrick's eyes, and he grimaced while cursing his anger. Blinking away the pain from his eyes, he failed to notice another guard coming up from behind to hook a pickaxe down at his leg irons. Then he felt himself falling forward and onto the dead salamander. Instantly the bullwhip of guard Schwartz went to work, lashing down to gouge out flesh and leave long welts seeping blood.

"That's your noon chow, boy!" Now he held back his whip arm. "Get with it, McKitrick, get to chowing down, boy."

Managing to spin onto his side, Wade McKitrick cast wild eyes out at the nearby terrain. A crazed thought came: maybe this was just a setup. He was out here breaking his back only because a message had been smuggled into prison that he volunteer for this work detail. The gist of it was that by his doing so it would make it easier for some concerned people to effect an escape. Right off McKitrick knew his brothers wouldn't scrawl such fancy words on paper, or others belonging to the McKitrick gang scattered to hell and gone by now. So what could he do, facing a life sentence with specifics from the sentencing judge he not be eligible for parole, at least not until Wade McKitrick was a couple of centuries older, and, further words from that judge, not a helluva lot wiser.

"Boy!"

The bullwhip lashing out put a painful emphasis upon the guard's mocking voice.

"Start chowing down, smartmouth! Or we could claim you was attempting to escape and just put a lot of bullets where the sun don't shine. Do it, boy, do it now!"

Earlier in the week, gun-for-hire Frank Modahl and two others had tracked in from the north. Modahl hailed out of that Sweetgrass country up near Harlowtown, had just been let go by a rancher up there for being overly ambitious with a running iron, among other things. Then, after drifting into Bozeman and a futile crack at its gaming tables, he'd lucked into this job.

And earlier in the week westward progress on the Union Pacific line had been in more open country, which had delayed the hardcases' attempt to break-out prisoner Wade McKitrick. But waiting had always been part of Frank Modahl's life, though the others were chomping at the bit to get this over with. Laying squinting eyes down the long barrel of his Winchester, Modahl reached up with his thumb and tipped his weathered hat back. He hawked out tobacco juice to have some of it blow against the stubbled cheek of his blocky face, with the north-westerly wind yammering out of a clear sky.

They had left their horses, and a spare one for McKitrick, down in the hollows just to the north, and to go on foot up this rocky elevation overlooking the railroad right-of-way. At a couple of hundred yards they were out of sixgun range, but it would be easy pickings for their rifles.

"You think them blue-bellies will have any horses in them railroad cars?"

"Reckon not, Petrie," responded Frank Modahl. "So once we have McKitrick we'll be home free."

"All of them prisoners look alike—mangy beards and worn down. Gonna be damned hard knowing which one is McKitrick."

"Wonder what that guard is fixin' to do with that salamander?"

"Don't know . . . but he's sure enough handy

11

with that bullwhip."

Frank Modahl tracked his rifle barrel after the guard calling out to some prisoners. The train whistle sounding flicked his eyes that way, back to the guard tossing the dead salamander at the feet of a prisoner. McKitrick, he heard the guard yell. And Modahl watched with amused eyes as Wade McKitrick was knocked off his feet, and Modahl said, "There's our boy."

"What are we waiting for?"

"Just wondering how hungry McKitrick is." And a belly laugh rumbled out of Frank Modahl. While his thoughts took a northward turn to Bozeman and a framed picture he'd been shown of the McKitrick brothers and some Montana politician.

There they'd been, the McKitricks, notorious gunfighters and killers, all duded up in suits and derbys, one seated to either side of Johnston Petti-grew, Wade McKitrick standing proudlike behind. Whilst Tanner McKitrick had a full black beard and the benevolent eyes of a preacher, the others, Wade and Blaine, had trim black mustaches and high cheekbones touching upon slate-gray eyes. Though not as famous as the Wild Bunch, the McKitricks had blazed crooked trails chiefly up in Wyoming and Montana, with a sojourn or two into Canada to make some bank withdrawals.

As for Frank Modahl's opinion of the brothers McKitrick, there was this growing urge to take on any of them in a sixgun showdown. For the more he'd studied that picture the more it came to Modahl that he didn't like any of the McKitricks. Maybe it was the arrogant tilt to Wade McKitrick's head or those mocking eyes, or just that by killing

Wade or another McKitrick he'd be enhancing his own reputation. But first there was the immediate concern of getting to the job at hand.

"Come on, boy, get to eating! I know your stomach is rubbing against your yellow backbone, McKitrick!"

Wade McKitrick threw up a protective arm when the guard's bullwhip sang out again, to have the biting thongs wrap around his upper neck and head. Then, to his disbelief, blood began bubbling out of Damon Schwartz's mouth and the man began sagging downward. While others scattered away from the heavy pounding of rifles opening up at the other guards, and a few soldiers foolhardy enough to venture away from the idling train. Off to McKitrick's left a guard dropped to his knees and brought up his rifle, only to have Wade McKitrick scramble up from the gravel-strewn ground and kick the man alongside the head. Grabbing the rifle, McKitrick worked the lever on the Spencer and fired from the hip at two soldiers heading for a jumbled pile of rocks, and as one of the soldiers flopped down to wiggle spasmodically, another prisoner clapped McKitrick on the back and exclaimed, "Damned good shooting! McKitrick, I'm breaking out with you."

Wordlessly, and as if he hadn't heard what the other prisoner said, Wade McKitrick broke running over a rail and up an exposed embankment. He kept on running awkwardly even as lead slugs chipped rocks and ground around him. Something stung into his left thigh but in the excitement of the moment he ignored the passing bite of the bullet while ducking behind a boulder, and from there to work his way up to one of the ambushers.

"You Wade McKitrick?"

"I'm McKitrick. About time you got here."

"No need gettin' hostile about it," Frank Modahl muttered as he eased away from the rock shelving. "What you bring him along for?"

"He came on his own invite."

"Too bad . . . since we've only got one spare horse."

"Yup," gasped Wade McKitrick. Sagging against a limber pine, he took a short breather. His torso was covered with sweat mingling with dust, and with his face having that ugly look of a man getting ready to use the rifle he carried.

Uneasily the other prisoner shrugged with his arms and said, "Don't matter none to me if I've gotta hoof it out of here. Obliged for getting me out . . . boys . . . and reckon I'll just be on my way . . ." He took off at a fast walk for a small copse of trees, and in them brought his stride into a downhill run, tearing around what shrubbery and mossy-clad rocks there was.

"Guess we won't have to worry about him," said Modahl. He jerked a thumb northward. "The horses are up there, McKitrick."

"I hope so," he replied, and bringing up the rifle, centered in on the other prisoner just touching upon a short section of level ground beyond which a creek beckoned. The one bullet from Wade McKitrick's rifle punched into the man's head to open it up like an overripe pumpkin.

"No need for that," said Modahl.

14

"Just wanted to see if the feel was still there," he said laconically.

"You're a cold one, awright."

"Where do we go from here?"

"We're cutting back to Montana. Brought some clothes along . . . and this." Down by the horses, Frank Modahl sidled up to a bronc and from a saddlebag he removed an envelope sealed with wax and tossed it at McKitrick along with a vague smile.

His eyes narrowing, Wade McKitrick tore open the envelope. Out tumbled a safety deposit box key and a folded piece of yellow paper upon which these cryptic words were boldly scrawled—"five thousand dollars has been deposited in your name at the First National Bank in Deadwood. Further instructions await you there, Mr. McKitrick."

When Wade McKitrick looked back at Frank Modahl, it was to find that the hardcase was saddlebound as were his companions, who had drawn their sixguns, and with Modahl saying, "I hope we'll run into one another again."

"Should I take him out, Frank?"

"Nope. Reckon McKitrick will have enough troubles once they come looking for him."

"Can't ride adorned with these leg irons," spat out Wade McKitrick.

"Sidesaddle you can," laughed Modahl, and then he spurred away.

Standing there, the contempt he felt for these men gleaming in his eyes, Wade McKitrick watched the hardcases lope into a draw. The horse left for him, a grulla, didn't have all that much of a bottom to it, and it was somewhat small, which meant to McKitrick that if he had any hopes of getting to the Black Hills he would have to set an easy pace.

"Easy," he mumbled, as working his way around the hind quarters of the grulla, he opened one of the saddlebags to remove a shapeless black hat and longsleeved shirt, bright blue and torn at the elbows, and Levis. The other saddlebag was empty. "Modahl, I know I'll run into you again."

About Wade McKitrick was this ability to handle most any situation. First he spread his legs apart, then after levering a shell into the breach of his Spencer, he lowered the muzzle until it almost touched the chain linking the leg irons and pulled the trigger. One link sprang apart, the slug punching into the rocky ground, the echoing report of his rifle carrying southward. Donning the shirt and hat, he thrust the pair of Levis back into a saddlebag, and cursed his anger because there was no boot for his rifle.

In the saddle, the Spencer cradled in his lap, Wade McKitrick set a northeasterly course. It would take a couple of days, he figured, for word to reach the territorial prison about his breakout. In all probability a telegram would be sent to army posts scattered around Wyoming, and to the cowtowns. To get to Deadwood the most logical route would be to skirt the Rattlesnakes and make his way along the Shoshone Basin.

"Maybe so," he pondered.

By striking that way, however, there was little doubt in his mind that he'd run into any number of cavalrymen out looking for him. Or even a cowtown sheriff or U.S. marshal. This time they'd be playing for keeps, and Wade McKitrick had no intentions of going back to prison. Of more immediate concern was getting hell and gone from this barren spot and ridding himself of these leg irons, and some corn whiskey wouldn't hurt either or a steak smothered in fried potatoes and onions.

The outlaw nighted along the Sweetwater River, a cold and lonely camp. With the grulla tethered nearby, Wade McKitrick sat with his back hunkered against a fallen cottonwood. He'd wrapped the saddle blanket around his shoulders to help ward off the encroaching chill, a lonely man craving a Mex cigarette, a man trying to figure out who was behind his prison-break. But someone out of Montana. Another hunk of these Great Plains where McKitrick and his brothers were known as wanted men.

One name kept hammering at his thoughts: Johnston Pettigrew. Pettigrew and the McKitricks had been partners in a sweet con game up at Bozeman. But when things began falling apart, all it took was a word from Pettigrew to the local law to have Wade McKitrick and his brothers head out fanning back leaden slugs and words of revenge. They'd split up upon riding into territorial Wyoming, and it was here that Wade McKitrick found himself looking down the barrel of a U.S. marshal's sixgun up at Sheridan.

"But Johnston Pettigrew sure as sin wouldn't bust me out of prison!"

He tried snuggling deeper into the saddle blanket reeking with the stench of horse, and then for some unknown reason another name wormed out of the bitter edges of his memory.

"Farnsworth . . . Lydel Farnsworth?"

17

Farnsworth money had backed up that enterprise in Bozeman. A rancher and businessman, Lydel Farnsworth had had a falling out with Pettigrew, and shortly afterwards, this according to Pettigrew, Farnsworth had threatened to tell what he knew to the law. There was also the fact Farnsworth's wife had been keeping more than casual company with Johnston Pettigrew. Still, doubt lingered in the thoughts of Wade McKitrick, as he knew Lydel Farnsworth to be a man with little backbone. Casting his thoughts further back into time, McKitrick knew a few others had sworn to gun down him and his brothers. That being the case, it would have happened this past noon, and by Frank Modahl.

"That five thousand waiting for me in Deadwood? With the money should be paper telling me who's behind this. That is, if I make it that far."

Despite a shutter banging incessantly against the wall of the blacksmith shop and dust scudding in the open door, Carbon County Sheriff Miles Treadway couldn't tear his eyes away from the dead smitty sprawled out on the floor.

What he and his deputy had pieced together was this, that the killer had ridden into Hanna sometime last night. Whereupon he had roused blacksmith Erik Jorgenson out of bed at gunpoint, most probably, then forced Jorgenson to get his forge going. Once this had been accomplished, the smitty had removed the leg irons but at considerable pain to Wade McKitrick.

"Then McKitrick tied up Jorgenson before going in and using a butcher knife on Jorgenson's wife."

18

"Came back here and burned out Jorgenson's eyes"—the deputy's boot nudged against a discarded pair of thongs—"with this. Then McKitrick stuck the barrel of his sixgun in Jorgenson's mouth and finished the job."

Pain radiated away from Sheriff Treadway's angry eyes. "And McKitrick still had gall enough to avail himself of Jorgenson's food and bed last night before pulling out. Probably changed clothes too."

"We sure it's Wade McKitrick?"

"Only a McKitrick could kill like this."

"Yeah, only Wade McKitrick. Damn, but I want him, Jim, bad. But no rope this time or hauling his rotten ass off to jail. Just a slow fire and a branding iron . . . same's he did to the smitty."

"I'd best fetch the undertaker."

"Yeah," the sheriff said wearily, "you do that. Whilst I mosey down to the Western Union office."

"You figure on tracking after McKitrick?"

"This damned wind will probably wipe out his trail. I figure he's hightailing it down into Colorado. Just hope we catch him before somebody else does . . . as I want to see justice served proper this time."

Chapter Two

The cowtown of Squaw Gap was snuggled in the western reaches of the Dakota Badlands, the winds reaching it whipping out of Montana as did the main line of the Northern Pacific Railroad. A sign planted along the outskirts of town and on the old stagecoach road passing southward toward the Black Hills told of Squaw Gap having a population of 201. The sign was weathered and faded out, the town considerably smaller now. A friendly and closeknit town, Squaw Gap owed its existence to the ranchers and the railroad. About all it could brag on was that Wild Bill Hickok had overnighted here on Hickok's way down to Deadwood. There were the usual Saturday night fights, at the saloons and mostly at Moseby's Dance Emporium and some petty thievery. But there'd been no killings in Squaw Gap. This was the way locals wanted it, just folks they knew coming in to shop or visit and the passenger and freight trains passing through daily.

The houses were scattered on both sides of the east-west running tracks on a wide tract of level ground, with Barcome Street to the south and all of the business places strung along it. Among the early settlers when this place had been just a few shanties and holding pens strung along the right-of-way had been Doc Don B. Barcome. His shingle still graced one of the older buildings on the street using his surname, something he had grudgingly approved. The street was wider than most, since, for as long as most locals could remember, there'd been talk of putting in a fountain and flower garden in the middle of it and rechristening it Barcome Boulevard, which some hoped would bring in more settlers. But somewhere along the line this idea had died out.

Unlike the neighboring town of Medora located under the lip of a high butte, and which lay about forty miles eastward, the land around Squaw Gap had a more gentle sweep to it, the meadows flowing away covered with thick verdant prairie grass, and some flowers. There were natural flowing wells, and here and there showed a windmill, and with Horse Head Creek oxbowing in from the southeast. Beyond the cottonwood and elm trees spilled amongst the buildings could be seen the shimmering heights of rugged buttes.

One of the traditions started by Doc Barcome was the annual Fourth of July celebration. Perhaps this was due to the doctor having served with the Union Army as one of its surgeons during the bloody Civil War. Graying now, but still an important part of things in Squaw Gap, Doc Barcome was a permanent fixture on the city council, and at the moment he'd just stepped under the arcade passing in front of the Claremont Hotel. What gave him pause was the sight of a newcomer to Squaw Gap, a man claiming to be a drifting preacher, turning the corner upstreet by Olivetti's Feed Store and coming this way.

Once the rough edges had worn off, the townspeople, along with Doc Barcome, had taken a liking to Thaddeus Beecher. Just last weekend Beecher had presided over the pulpit at St. Thomas Evangelical Church, and he certainly looked the part, mused Barcome, clothed as Thaddeus Beecher was in black frock coat and matching trousers, unspurred boots and stiff white shirt, these articles of clothing draped over Beecher's tall and gaunt frame. While the full black beard marked with a white streak flaring down the left cheekbone and severe flat-crowned black hat were offset by kindly blue eyes, the occasional smile showing bony-white teeth. Another daily protuberance was the leather-bound bible Thaddeus Beecher had tucked under an arm.

As Doc Barcome stood there, the mayor of Squaw Gap thrust his upper body out of an open window and said, "Time's a-wasting, Doc. Besides, I've got some exciting news . . . so hustle in here."

Moving on, Doc Barcome went through the lobby door, and from there veered over to another which brought him into the dining room and a large table occupied by members of the city council, and also in attendance was Rain Lonigan, Squaw Gap's temporary marshal. Draping his hat on a coat rack, he found a chair at the table and an empty cup.

Filling the cup with coffee, Rain Lonigan said, "Doc, you look kind of peaked."

"Just old age creeping up on him," smiled Ray Oberlander.

"Enough chitchat," Mayor Armond Weaver said impatiently. "Well, gents, he's accepted our invitation to speak here on the Fourth of July."

22

"Now who might that be, Armond?"

"Doggonit, Earl, you know good and well I'm talking about one of Montana's most famous politicians . . . the honorable Johnston Pettigrew."

Dropping a couple of lumps of sugar into his cup, Doc Barcome said quietly, "He was just funning you, Armond. And just what kind of fee does the honorable Johnston Pettigrew expect for his appearance in our humble little town?"

"Doc, not a blasted thin dime. Seems Pettigrew will be passing through on his way to Washington City. Gents, this is an opportunity we cannot afford to pass up. Why, when Earl there, writes this up in his newspaper folks'll come from miles around just to catch a glimpse of Pettigrew. Not to mention what this'll mean for the city coffers." The telegram held by the mayor fluttered erratically as he spoke.

"Not to mention this should help you get reelected."

"Well, gents, all in favor of responding to Pettigrew's telegram raise your hands. Good . . . good . . . and which means we'll really have to spiffy up the streets. Banners and bunting and such."

"There ain't a whole helluva lot in the city coffers, mayor."

"Let's not quibble over mere pennies when all of us know come the Fourth of July we'll more than pay for any expenses incurred."

"Suppose you're right," said Doc Barcome. He turned inquiring eyes upon Rain Lonigan. "Checked on Arty Greenway this morning; he'll be laid up for at least another ten days. Hope your filling in as town marshal won't keep you away from your ranch all that much."

"About all I've done so far is watch the moss grow on the water tank over at Gintley's livery stable."

"There was a fight Saturday night at the dance hall."

"Nothing much to it, Earl. Just a scuffle between two drunken waddies."

"I assume you told them to head out."

"I did, mayor."

"In the past this has been Marshal Greenway's policy," went on Mayor Weaver. "Perhaps a night in jail and a stiff fine could end this sort of thing."

"The ranchers like things the way they are," said editor Earl Paulson. "We rile them up . . . they just might tell those working for them to spend their time and money at Medora . . . or Sentinel Butte."

"Still, gents, times are changing. Every day passenger trains pass through carrying settlers by the hundred. Won't be too much longer before uncivilized ways go the way of the buffalo and such."

"Until then, mayor," broke in Doc Barcome, "let's not evoke too many changes for Squaw Gap. We're a peaceable, take your time kind of cowtown. And by the way, Rain, mean to drop out and look in on your wife."

"So far Jillian's been doing fine—but you never know about a woman fixin' to have a baby."

This was followed by small talk and a few items brought up by city clerk Ben Oberlander, a paunchy man with cherubic features. Then the meeting broke up, with Rain Lonigan leaving first.

He spent the remainder of the afternoon at the marshal's office, sweeping up and making sure the fire was out in the pot-bellied stove, the big blackened coffee pot washed out, before he left to head over to Gintley's and claim his gelding.

When Rain Lonigan rode out of Squaw Gap, it was along a southern track worn by heavy usage. His spread, the Rocking L, lay about five miles out, a smaller ranch upon which Lonigan raised around three hundred cattle. As for the rancher, Rain Lonigan was of average height at five-ten, but he looked somewhat younger than his twenty-five years. He had dark brown hair, had started to show a few crinkles around his smoky-gray eyes. Out at the ranch the holstered Peacemaker would be hung on a wall peg in the back porch of his small ranchhouse. The Lonigans had two children, the boy Kiley, and his older sister, Sara. And it was of some concern to Rain Lonigan that another child was on the way. Cattle prices hadn't been all that high the last couple of years, which was the major reason he'd taken this temporary job as town marshal. But on the brighter side of things was the fact June had brought more rain than usual. Adding to this was Jillian Lonigan, his wife of five years and a woman of unusual patience.

"About all the woman a man could want," was Rain Lonigan's quiet comment as his questing eyes swept southwesterly to an area infested with low boggy spots lying along a creek. While the home buildings were located about a mile beyond where the creek dipped to the north.

When he passed beneath the streaked side of a bluff, one of the dogs began yowling, then the other one, and a smile shone in Rain Lonigan's eyes when Sara pranced out from behind rose bushes planted in front of the one-story log house. As he rode that way, Rain's son darted out onto the front porch and yelled, "Pa, Sara's been pulling my hair . . . and . . . and calling me sissy names."

"That so, little daughter," said Rain as he swung down.

"Oh, Kiley's such a baby. Won't leave my dolls alone."

"Don't tell me you've taken to playing with dolls, Kiley Lonigan." Around his laughter Rain Lonigan had time to ruffle his son's hair as the front door opened to have his wife step out while wiping her hands on the checkered apron.

"Glad you're home, dear."

Still holding the reins, he came in close to the open porch railing, and as Jillian Lonigan leaned his way, they kissed. "Doc Barcome said it would be another ten days before Greenway's up and around."

"That means," she said with some concern, "you'll still be wearing that badge during the Fourth of July celebration."

"Now, Jillian, don't fret about that. I'll deputize two or three men. And guess what? Seems our little town is going to have a celebrity here for the Fourth—this Johnston Pettigrew. Some Montana politician."

"That should prove interesting."

"Oh, Doc Barcome's coming out."

"Rain, you know we can't afford these visits."

"What we can't afford is to take any chances.

26

Getting on sundown. I expect Casey is in."

"Caught a glimpse of him coming in about an hour ago. Probably down at the barn." Jillian Lonigan placed a lingering hand on her husband's smoothly-shaven face, while in her widely-spaced eyes there was a soft glow. Her pregnancy was very much in evidence despite the covering apron. Her auburn hair hung well down her slender back, her bosom was full, the face of Jillian Lonigan somewhat tanned and without any makeup.

"Well, tend to your horse, Rain, while I tend to my cooking. And you children, head around back and wash up for supper. And, Sara, quit pulling your brother's hair. Scat, now."

Back of the house where a pole corral stood overlooking a dropoff below which a creek showed muddy waters, Rain Lonigan unsaddled the gelding as his only hand, whiskery and somewhat cantankerous Casey Tessler, emerged from the barn. Tessler ambled over on bowed legs and said, "Some of those bog holes are drying up. But I pulled out a couple. How's things in Squaw Gap?"

"Same as always."

"How much longer this marshaling job gonna last?"

"Only ten more days, I'm hoping."

Lifting his hat away from his graying hair, Casey Tessler used the same hand to scratch at his long sideburn as he said, "I'll get some hay cut by then, Rain. Shore is thick this year. That preacher fella still hanging around town?"

"Beecher? Yup, he's still there."

Casey Tessler fell silent as the man he worked for turned the gelding loose in the corral, but once they fell into step on their way toward the house, Tessler murmured ponderingly, "Thaddeus Beecher? Somehow that name don't ring true . . ."

"Meaning Beecher isn't a preacher?"

"You know I've been a lot of places, Rain. Worked clear across Colorado and away up into Montana. May be gettin' somewhat old and not so clear about a lot of things . . . but it's there . . . this notion I've seen this sky pilot a-fore. And usin' a different name."

"I'm sure it'll come to you."

"Yup, forget some things . . . but that sweet smell coming out of the kitchen sure picks up a man after a hard day's riding."

He clapped Casey Tessler on the shoulder. "For sure there's nothing wrong with your nose."

"Or this belly of mine."

"Casey, getting back to this preacher, you think he's here just to pull some flim-flam game . . ."

"From what I hear he can preach a helluva sermon. Maybe I'm just barking up the wrong tree about Thaddeus Beecher. Still . . . I get this feeling about him sometimes . . . sort of like a coyote loping over someone's grave."

Chapter Three

Up in his room at the Starbuck Hotel the man known as Thaddeus Beecher uncorked the bottle and poured corn whiskey into a glass. He brought the glass over to a window and laid disinterested eyes upon two men putting up a platform out in the middle of Barcome Street. Every so often the constant wind would pick up dusty ground and spiral it along the street, and at times he could hear the wooden building he was in creak protestingly or window panes rattle. About three days ago the wind had started howling out of Montana along with the temperature climbing into the high nineties. But it was the wind he hated, for it seemed to have a bedeviling mind all its own, never seeming to let up, always hammering at a man be he in a no-account town like this or out on the plains.

"Three more days."

They'd be trailing in from the Black Hills, Wade and Blaine, and maybe three or four more. It was down in western Nebraska that he'd learned of Wade's being arrested and sent to the territorial prison at Rawlins. Just a stroke of bad luck, he mused. As for his other brother, Blaine, the last Thaddeus Beecher had heard, Blaine was in Dodge City, bucking the tiger and living with a whore named Billie O'Day. Well, Blaine was no saint and this whore was about as Irish as that tumbleweed dancing downstreet. Then came the startling news Wade McKitrick had busted out of prison, this gleaned from a letter sent by Wade, and that he should make tracks for Deadwood.

And it was in Deadwood that the McKitrick brothers had a quiet reunion. They'd sequestered themselves at the Merchant's Hotel, which boasted in Deadwood newspapers that it had forty-five well-furnished rooms, billiard parlors and sample rooms, and the finest dining room in the Black Hills. It was in one of the three barrooms that Tanner McKitrick was asked to don his garb as a preacher and head up north to a place called Squaw Gap. And his response to Wade McKitrick had been rather curt, "Pious and whiskey don't mix, brother."

"Maybe so, brother Tanner. But someone went to considerable expense to bust me out of territorial prison."

"Seven thousand is a lot of working capital."

"We kill Johnston Pettigrew and we'll have another seven thousand to split three ways."

"No question that I won't be sorry when Pettigrew goes down. But you still haven't told me who's bankrolling this thing?"

Wade McKitrick allowed a wry smile to show as he riffled a deck of cards and fanned them out face up. "Dammit, Tanner," he said easily, "I don't know. All I found in that safety deposit box was the seven thousand and a promise that amount would be matched if we killed Pettigrew."

"Promises are like farting in the wind," intoned Tanner McKitrick.

"And that Pettigrew would be spouting off at a place called Squaw Gap come the Fourth of July." He added hotly, "That bastard owes us."

Blaine McKitrick, who'd been eyeing one of the bar girls, said, "All Pettigrew was was a snake oil salesman. Had a good thing going up there at Bozeman. Then he got rattled and turned the law on us."

"Seems to me," said Wade McKitrick, "it was Pettigrew's partner who ran scared first."

"Yeah, Lydel Farnsworth." Tanner McKitrick's teeth showed in a thoughtful grimace. "Maybe it wasn't so much that Farnsworth wanted to keep clear of things. Just that he wanted to get back at Johnston Pettigrew because of Pettigrew playing up sweet to his wife. As I recollect, Mrs. Ella Farnsworth was some handsome kind of woman. Was me, brothers, I wouldn't mind tucking my Justons under her bed."

"Oh, hell," said Blaine McKitrick, "we've got the seven thousand . . . and Wade, you're out of jail. What the hell, let's make tracks down south for a spell. Texas or Old Mexico?"

"Tempting, Blaine, damned tempting," said Wade McKitrick. "You boys ever hear of a two-bit gunslick name of Frank Modahl—"

Tanner McKitrick, graying and somewhat older than his brothers, lowered his elbows onto the arms of his chair. At times like this he was prone to let his left eyelid down a little, a sign to his brothers that there was indeed a moment of recollection. His bony left hand reached out for the glass of whiskey, brought it to his lips. Instead of allowing the corn whiskey to settle into his stomach, Tanner

31

McKitrick swilled it around in his mouth, his way of cleansing his teeth, and then he spat the mouthful of whiskey down at sawdust and muttered sonorously, "You remember Buster Graybone?"

"Let's see . . ."

"It was down in Colorado?" ventured Wade McKitrick.

Piously Tanner McKitrick said, "It was Buster Graybone and some others including Frank Modahl that tried to take out this bank at Kings Canyon, you know, down in Colorado. Got in there with no problem. Coming out it was to find every able-bodied man in town peppering away with a gun. So when Modahl's horse got hit, he shot Graybone out of the saddle. Took off on Graybone's horse. Frank Modahl was the only one to get out of there alive."

"Modahl about left me afoot out there," groused Wade McKitrick. "Lucky for me I was able to grab a rifle breaking out or he might have gunned me down. As it was I had a helluva time making it to Deadwood."

"From the way you're belting that whiskey down, Wade, it appears you're going through with this."

"Yup, Tanner, I am. Farnsworth's got to be behind this. First we take out Johnston Pettigrew. Then we strike back to Bozeman and get reacquainted with Mr. Lydel Farnsworth. This seven thousand front money ain't near enough. Or that other seven thousand we get for killing Pettigrew. Just could be, brothers, we'll end up owning that ranch Farnsworth is always bragging on. Either that or Farnsworth winds up decorating a burial plot."

Those last words of Wade McKitrick's had been greeted with silent approval by his brothers. Shortly afterward Tanner McKitrick had caught a north-bound stage. "And here I be," he remarked wryly, "pining away in Squaw Gap."

During the two and a half weeks he'd been here, Tanner McKitrick had looked over the layout, of the town and the railroad depot and its connecting environs, the way the depot lay out in the open, and a likely ambush spot the holding pens just eastward. He'd even considered the possibility of stopping the train before it reached Squaw Gap. But just killing Johnston Pettigrew wouldn't ensure the McKitricks getting away cleanly.

So, as he stared again at the platform being erected just upstreet from the hotel, he knew this was where they would do the killing. The train was scheduled to arrive at exactly 11:00 in the morning of the Fourth. Waiting at the depot would be some Squaw Gap dignitaries and a marching band comprised of locals. From there everyone would sashay over to the Squaw Gap Social Club for vittles. Then around one o'clock the blowhards, as Thaddeus Beecher called them, would congregate on the platform taking up considerable space out in the middle of the street for some patriotic oratory. The afternoon's activities included some sporting events for the children of Squaw Gap, a baseball game, a rodeo.

"Only thing is," he said piously, "blood's gonna flow before that afternoon gets a chance to set in. Amen, brother." Through a pleased smile he toasted his reflection in the window pane. Then he emptied the glass and set it aside, reached for his flat-crowned hat and by force of habit, the worn leather-bound Bible.

Down in the lobby, he tipped his hat to a couple of bustled women chattering magpielike as they headed for the dining room, neither of whom cast a second glance at Thaddeus Beecher drifting through the open front door, where he paused for a moment under the covered arcade. This acting the role of drifting sky pilot was wearing on him, but with just three more days until his brothers rode in, he could tolerate matters here in Squaw Gap. One of the things he'd done was to cultivate the friendships of those people who he judged would have some bearing on the upcoming festivities. Ben Oberlander, the city clerk, had been less guarded about talking to Thaddeus Beecher after catching one of his sermons, and with Oberlander's son, Marcus, showing up at unexpected times to tag along whenever the drifting preacher took one of his frequent strolls around town. The boy was more a nuisance than anything, mused Tanner McKitrick, who couldn't recall the last time he'd spoken to much less tolerated yonkers.

Tanner McKitrick's purpose in leaving the hotel just as the sun was edging down upon western-lying buttes was an invitation to attend a bake sale over at the social club. He likened this to taking a bath, an infrequent event in his lonely, drifting life. He was expected to lead them in prayer before partaking of an evening meal. There was also an ulterior motive for his accepting this invitation, and that was a young widow woman living on the edge of town. A couple of years ago, he'd been told, Dalphine Wickland's husband had been gored by a

34

bull, died before the local sawbones could get out there. Now Dalphine Wickland took in washing and also waited on tables in the dining room of the Starbuck Hotel, which was where he'd engaged her in conversation from time to time. She was somewhat young, not more than thirty, comely, and from long experience Tanner McKitrick sensed that behind the shy countenance lurked a lusting nature. The trick, as he saw it, was to wrangle an invitation to her house. Once there, nature would take its wanton course.

"Out for some evening air, Reverend Beecher?"

He swung sideways to glimpse the editor of the *Squaw Gap Chronicle* coming along the boardwalk in that slouching way he had, the coat thrown carelessly over his shoulders and ink staining the rumpled gray shirt. In a way he liked Earl Paulson, though the editor seemed rather aloof whenever they encountered one another on the streets.

"I expect you wrote a front page story about the impending visit of . . . of this politician from Montana . . . yes, this Pettigrew fellow . . ."

"The story practically wrote itself, Beecher. Consider this headline—Montana Politician Extends Heat Wave At Squaw Gap." They laughed together, and Earl Paulson went on with, "Not that I'm against Johnston Pettigrew speaking here during the Fourth. Just that I hope it cools into the seventies. Perchance, Beecher, you're going over to the social club?"

"The reason, sir, I'm venturing out on this hot street. This wind has my equal disdain."

"Yes, as it does mine. Where did you say you preached last?"

"My dear Mr. Paulson, preaching has carried me to all points of the compass. God's work is never done, I'm afraid."

"How true." Passing onto a side street, Earl Paulson nodded at a passing couple as he veered over and opened one of the doors leading into a large, boxy building with whitewashed walls and a peaked roof. He entered after Thaddeus Beecher, who gave the editor a pleasant nod of dismissal.

"I believe, Mr. Paulson, I shall tarry here for a moment. To savor the tangy odors of cooking."

Doffing his hat, Paulson replied, "Do the same thing when I enter a saloon; force of habit." He sauntered from the entryway into the main hall and eased to some locals.

Turning, Thaddeus Beecher put his hat with others resting on one of the shelves, but he still retained the Bible as he strode slowly into the hall and looked around. Then he spotted Dalphine Wickland just coming out of the large kitchen to the rear of the building, and upon sighting Beecher, there appeared a tentative smile, to which he responded. Within the half-hour most of the men and some ladies in attendance had settled down at tables set in two straight lines with chairs to either side. The mayor's wife waved him down to the back end of one of her tables, where she said loudly, "Please, everyone, supper's ready. So please be seated." She turned beaming eyes upon Thaddeus Beecher. "I just want to tell you, Reverend Beecher, just how exciting it is to listen to you preach. Fire and brimstone, I call it."

"The power of the Lord comes upon me at times," he responded. "Folks, you have a truly enchanting town. Squaw Gap—now there's a name that will long endure out here in these beautiful Badlands. Someday it shall be famous for more than just that Wild Bill Hickok stayed here." He smiled as everyone applauded. "Now, folks, be so kind as to bow your heads in prayer."

"Reverend Beecher, I can't believe you asked to walk me home."

"Thaddeus will do . . . that is, if I can call you Dalphine."

"Please, do."

The last glow of the sun was barely showing in a sky becoming etched with stars. Hanging low to the northeast was a silvery moon, and to Thaddeus Beecher's intense relief the wind which had been plaguing Squaw Gap for almost a week had died away. She strolled to his left, and now he crooked out his elbow and said, "Please, I might lose you in the dark."

Laughing, Dalphine Wickland said, "How sweet of you . . . Thaddeus."

"It mystifies me that an attractive woman such as yourself hasn't gotten married again . . . at least after two years."

"Perhaps it's because good men are hard to find," she said pensively. "Or perhaps it was because I didn't want to marry another cowhand. Some came courting, you know."

"That is a rather uncertain life."

"What about you, Thaddeus, don't you get tired of this . . . drifting from town to town?"

"It wearies me, I can say truthfully. But for me

to settle in one place would be more wearying."

"Yes, I can understand that. Especially here in Squaw Gap."

"Well, is this your charming abode?"

"All that I salvaged from my marriage." They slipped in under some elm trees looming over the short walkway. At the front porch, Dalphine Wickland smiled uneasily. "I . . . that was nice, Thaddeus."

"You have your house. And I have the lonely sanctuary of my room back at the hotel. And the night's so young, restive . . ."

"Would you . . . care to come in for a cup of coffee, Thaddeus?"

"I trust I wouldn't be intruding."

"No," she said quickly, "not at all."

"Only one, then." He followed her up the short flight of steps and into a small living room, and once a lamp had been lit, he placed his bible on the round table covered with a lacy tablecloth. "This is a very comfortable house, Dalphine."

"I'll . . . I'll throw some wood in the kitchen stove . . . get some coffee brewing."

He stepped toward the open door and watched her stoke the cast-iron stove, couldn't help noticing that she was all too aware of his presence, this in the nervous way she fussed with her auburn hair, and now a sidelong glance his way, and he said, "What holds you to Squaw Gap?"

"Habit, I suppose. Have you ever been married?"

"My wife passed away a long time ago. Just a faded tintype in my thoughts now." His eyes held those of Dalphine Wickland's. Now he could see the slight flicker of desire. Striding boldly toward her, he slipped a hand behind her head, pressed his lips hard to hers, could feel the woman trembling under the touch of his rough and seeking hands. "I want you."

"Thaddeus . . . no . . ."

He lifted her up and swung around and found a doorway leading into her bedroom. Lowering her to the bed, he murmured huskily, "I wanted you the first moment I set eyes on you, woman."

"As I do you . . . Thaddeus."

And with that no more words were spoken.

Chapter Four

The woman in the velvety blue dress lifted her eyes delicately from a copy of the *Montana Standard* as another carriage pulled up to the curbing. Once the driver had clambered down to open the carriage door for his passengers, an older couple, Ella Farnsworth reached somewhat anxiously for her cup and dropped her eyes to the newspaper again.

The various stories spread across the front page of the *Montana Standard* told her all she wanted to know. Of how a special train of the Northern Pacific Railroad, the North Coast Limited, had left Seattle several days ago to help celebrate the railroad's tenth anniversary. Aboard would be railroad officials, politicians and others on the North Coast Limited's run to St. Paul. Of the Montanans expected to make the long journey her interest lay only in the fact Johnston Pettigrew would be on the train. She knew that Pettigrew had been staying at Butte's Thornton Hotel, that he would be entraining for Washington City to pick up the reins as one of territorial Montana's newly elected representatives. Traveling with Pettigrew would be his latest conquest, and Ella Farnsworth murmured, "Just another hussy."

The booth she occupied in the crowded dining

room stood before a large window looking out onto bustling Silver Street. Other carriages were arriving, and the sidewalks were filled with people coming into the passenger station, some to purchase tickets, but most of them here to catch a glimpse of the famous North Coast Limited, which had arrived earlier in the day, and would depart within the half hour.

As for Ella Farnsworth, she had taken special pains with her appearance. Lamplight touched the glossy black iridescence of her raveny hair swept up under the dark blue hat plumaged with feathers. The violet eyes were watchful, but held a secretive glint, and there would be a return smile from full lips for the occasional gentlemen strolling past her booth. Ella's full bosom tapered down to a willowy waist, and the dress had long sleeves and swept to the floor. At her side in the booth was a matching coat and overnight case. In her purse there was also a ticket for the North Coast Limited.

"Yes, there he is," she exclaimed silently.

Just upstreet and in front of the station a hansom cab discharged Johnston Pettigrew and his female companion. Porters were there to take their luggage, while into the eyes of Ella Farnsworth slithered the true feelings she had for this man. She couldn't deny the fact Pettigrew was a very handsome man, perhaps too handsome for his own good, with that mane of blondish hair, the leonine features, the tall erect carriage. And a spellbinder of the first order. But she was one of the few people to know Johnston Pettigrew's true character, that a lie slid as easily through his wide lips as had the words that he loved Ella Farnsworth. Theirs had been a brief interlude of passion, and from Pettigrew, broken promises. This was what had fetched her away from Bozeman and westward to here, and something else, the pain of which still gripped her heart and thoughts.

To the satiny rustling of her dress Ella Farnsworth rose, retrieved her belongings, left the dining room and began crossing the interior court of the large station. People were crowding near the entrance gates, but her ticket gave her access to the train idling along the platform. She found the front vestibule of the observation car and the willing arm of a conductor.

"Have a good trip, ma'am."

Ella Farnsworth smiled. "I see extra cars have been added."

"Yes, ma'am — some tourist sleeping cars. But according to your ticket you have a compartment in the observation car."

"Some friends of mine came aboard . . . the Pettigrews . . ."

"Pettigrew . . . I believe they have compartment five."

From the vestibule Ella Farnsworth made her way back through the observation car. A corridor ran the length of the car, flanked upon one side by a series of compartments in the manner of hotel rooms. Doors connected each compartment, with the main corridor, and from either side by heavily mirrored doors. She let herself into compartment four, threw the door latch before placing her belongings on the narrow bed. The small but elegantly furnished stateroom contained, besides

42

the bed, a washstand with a wall mirror, an over-stuffed chair and hanging drapery, and the window covered by a red velvety curtain. Stepping back to a connecting door which opened onto stateroom five, she pressed an ear against the flowered door pane. At first she couldn't hear anything, then came the muffled voice of Johnston Pettigrew's woman of the moment.

Turning away, Ella removed her hat, and then she went to freshen up at the washstand. For a moment she gazed at her reflection in the mirror, from force of habit looking for those telltale age lines. She still considered herself a comely woman, as did most men she encountered in her few journeys away from Bozeman. But it wasn't Ella Farnsworth's hopes of meeting someone new that had brought her to Butte. Only what would happen on this train tonight.

Ella Farnsworth did not consider herself a woman scorned, since she was married when Johnston Pettigrew came into Bozeman and her life. Eagerly she'd thrown herself into Johnston's arms. For life with her husband had been just a dreary routine of Bozeman and the ranch. At this time her husband, Lydel, had invested heavily in a business venture started by Johnston Pettigrew. Only it turned out to be some con game run by Pettigrew and backed up by three outlaws, the McKitrick brothers. Then the killings started. As for Ella Farnsworth and her husband, they were on the verge of bankruptcy when the McKitricks were chased out of town and the blame for what happened pointed not at Pettigrew but her husband, Lydel. Johnston Pettigrew had left too, and months later she'd found out Pettigrew had taken up residence at Butte.

Only those with influence and political power would be on the North Coast Limited. There'd be gambling in the parlor cars, deals would be made and all of the drinks courtesy of the railroad. And Ella Farnsworth felt at ease, for aboard this train were the kind of people she'd rubbed elbows with most of her life. While tonight she must be at her charming best as the North Coast Limited made that hundred mile run eastward toward Bozeman and beyond.

The train lurching forward brought her thoughts away from Johnston Pettigrew and to her purse, which she picked up while taking a final look at herself in the mirror. She left the compartment and made her way forward to the dining car, to have a negro porter escort Ella to a table gleaming with silverware. From the printed menu she selected the saddle of veal, and as an appetizer, a glass of sherry. Others were drifting in, as through the wide windows flowed rugged landscape being plated in gold tints by the setting sun. The sherry came first, and then Johnston Pettigrew was there, settling down at a table occupied by another couple.

"Mr. Nordvall, I can't tell you how excited I am to be a part of this," said Johnston Pettigrew.

"We at the Northern Pacific thank you, sir. And you, young lady, have such delightful eyes." He returned Rose Dumont's pleased smile. "I've been told you two are getting married."

"My beautiful Rose has relatives in St. Paul. Immediately after the wedding ceremony it's off to Washington City."

"I hope you won't forget the Northern Pacific."

"Hardly that," replied Pettigrew as his eyes drifted deeper into the dining car. They settled in disbelief upon Ella Farnsworth. Resentment flooded through him, just a trace of unease, and there was no mistaking the invitation in the violet eyes gazing at him over the rim of her glass. She had no right to be here. Perhaps she'd taken a trip, was on her way back to Bozeman? Framing a smile for those at his table, Johnston Pettigrew murmured an apology, and rising, he went back to Ella's table.

"Johnston, what a delightful surprise."

"Yes, it has been some time. How are . . . things, in Bozeman?"

"Much better now."

"And your husband?"

"Lydel's doing just fine," she lied around a smile. "He's been restocking the ranch." As he sat down, Ella Farnsworth glanced at the vase of flowers on her table. "Such lovely roses. Do you recall sending me some . . ."

"You're still a beautiful and delightful woman, Ella."

"Perhaps at one time. So you're off to Washington City."

"First there'll be a stop at St. Paul. I'm . . . getting married."

"As you promised me you'd do one time. But really, Johnston, let's say it was one of those things. I suppose we all make mistakes."

"I'm pleased that you've forgiven me, Ella. Many a time I thought about you . . . and what might have been." He shrugged with his shoulders. "Perhaps it wasn't meant to be."

"She's lovely."

"And so very charming. I met Rose Dumont at Butte . . . and one thing led to another."

"Excuse me, folks," said the negro porter as he came up. "But we're terribly crowded, and these folks need a place to sit down."

Ella returned Pettigrew's smile as he stood up and moved back to his table. Then she exchanged small talk with the couple settling down at her table, even though inwardly burned a deep well of anger. She came up to Butte about two weeks ago and secured a room at a modest hotel. During this time she'd been checking on Johnston Pettigrew's daily activities, and it was then she found out about Pettigrew's intentions to get married. She also knew that he'd be aboard this train, but would leave it farther eastward in the Dakota Badlands, and at a cowtown named Squaw Gap.

"And for you, my beloved Johnston Pettigrew, the end of the line," came Ella Farnsworth's silent and chilling words.

When false dawn was gracing the Bridgers and Gallatins farther to the south, the North Coast Limited has just pulled into Bozeman to discharge a single passenger. The only signs of life were the depot agent and a cowhand alighting from a carriage. The cowhand, a jaded nod of greeting to Ella Farnsworth, picked up her luggage, and together they watched the passenger train slip away from the platform.

"How was your trip, Mrs. Farnsworth?"

She stood there without answering, because on that train Ella Farnsworth had found out she was capable of murder. It had been late, sometime past midnight, when she'd spotted Johnston Pettigrew and some others still playing poker, knew the game would continue for some time. And so at a hurried pace Ella had gone back to the observation car and her compartment.

Earlier in the evening she had slipped back and unlocked the door connecting her compartment to Pettigrew's. So it had been a simple matter to open the door, and with knife in hand, enter to gaze down at Rose Dumont stretched out on the bed she'd be sharing with Johnston Pettigrew. Even now Ella didn't know what had stayed her hand. But at the time the urge to lash out at Pettigrew had brought the hand holding the knife over her head. Blinded by a hatred so intense it had twisted up her face shrewishly, the knife had started down, only to have Ella Farnsworth by sheer force of will stop the killing thrust and back away. No, something in her had said, not now. Let them go on to Squaw Gap. For now let Johnston Pettigrew believe he would not be made to pay for what he'd done to her, and her husband.

"Yes . . . my trip? Fine. Toby, take my luggage to the carriage. I have to send a telegram." She crossed the wide platform and entered the depot office.

"That North Coast Limited is some train, Mrs. Farnsworth."

47

"A most exciting trip." From her purse she removed a folded sheet of paper and handed it to the depot agent.

Unfolding the paper, he read, "Let's see . . . for this Beecher gent over to Squaw Gap. That'll be six bits."

"I trust that telegram will be delivered before the train gets there?"

"Oh, shore, Mrs. Farnsworth, no problem there. And much obliged." He turned to the telegraph key as she went outside.

Cowhand Toby Mathers, around fifty but stooped so that he appeared to be considerably older, helped the woman he worked for climb into the carriage, and with Ella saying, "I want to see my husband."

Gimpylegging around the carriage, he found the front seat, grasped the reins in his leathered hands and brought the bay away from the depot along the street following the western flow of the tracks. A block later he swung onto another street angling mostly to the south. At this hour only a few early risers could be seen and once in a while window light. After passing a storage shed adorned with faded letters proclaiming it to be the property of the Midland Cartel Company, Mathers swung southwesterly onto a rutted lane. It was a little clearer now, and dew glistened on the carpeting of grass and filled the low spots but danced whitely in a stand of elm trees. As a picket fence appeared, he reined up and swung sideways on the seat. Gazing with some concern at Ella, he said, "Want me to go with you?"

"No, Toby," she replied as she left the carriage

to step slowly along the picket fence and pass through an open gate. Without too much difficulty she found Lydel Farnsworth's grave.

She lifted the shawl over her head, drew it closer around her neck, and through softening eyes Ella said. "You only miss a person when he's gone. Lydel . . . Lydel, how I let you down."

There came the painful and shocking memory of how she'd found her husband lying dead in the carriage house, a finger still wedged in the trigger guard of the shotgun. And later the note of apology in Lydel Farnsworth's study. With his death came the weeks of isolation and bitter self-condemnation. For Ella knew, but too late, that it was because she'd taken up with Johnston Pettigrew this had happened.

"Lydel . . . I know you can hear me. That you blame me for all that happened. But I swear, my dear husband, the day of reckoning is coming for Johnston Pettigrew . . . damn him."

Chapter Five

Behind Wade and Blaine McKitrick lay Black Butte set off by its lonesome just north of a long rocky plateau extending into the hazy distance. Back a piece a sodbuster had told them they'd reach the southern edges of the Badlands by noon, and a cowtown there called Marmouth. First the McKitricks and four other hardcases had taken a short breather amongst hills stippled with cedars, and upon loping on, to come upon the Little Missouri River sidewinding in the direction they were heading, that being due north.

Wade McKitrick knew it was the second day of July, so there was no need to hurry. This time he was riding a horse with plenty of bottom, and the saddle was new. When in the chips Wade McKitrick favored fancy clothes, such as what he had on now, black corduroy trousers, roweled spurs on his Texas boots, Peacemakers hanging at both hips but under a cattleman's leather coat, and a gray Stetson. In his saddlebags were extra bullets for both sideguns and the Winchester. Wade, like his brother, Blaine, had dark hawkish features, and with those manes of coal black hair hanging shaggy sometimes they were mistaken for being halfbloods. One who'd inquired about this, this being across the Rockies at Cody, never quite finished his sentence before Wade beat his brother to the draw and pumped three slugs into an area on the man's chest you could cover with a silver dollar. Unlike their brother Tanner, they had quicksilver tempers, surly mannerisms, but as Tanner McKitrick did, enjoyed killing more than gambling or womanizing.

With the McKitricks were two they'd ridden with before, Larry Madden, a lanky Texan and Brent Wilmar, who preferred to be called Will. The others were hardcases Wade McKitrick had taken on down at Deadwood, one known only as Smithly, and the other man a gold miner turned outlaw, Jesse Cairne. Smithly and Cairne were told only that they were heading north into the Badlands to kill someone. To Wade McKitrick these men were expendable, that if things didn't go as planned up at Squaw Gap, they'd be left behind.

"There's the river."

"Not holding much water . . . and muddy as hell."

"Heard there's a lot of quicksand along it."

"Expect there is," said Wade McKitrick.

"Want to take five?"

Blaine McKitrick said, "Can't be that far to Marmouth. We'll overnight there and press on in the morning."

Marmouth lay snugged among trees and alongside the Little Missouri. It had the one business street but without any boardwalks or shading porches. And just the one saloon, The Rover's Bar. Larry Madden's comment that the place

51

seemed awful dead brought a curt nod from Wade McKitrick, who swung down and squinted upward.

"Must be around four, or maybe after. Don't see any hotel."

"Must be some rooming houses," said Blaine as he tied his reins to the hitching rack. "But right now a drink'll set me up." Without waiting for the others he swaggered toward the open door and stepped inside to have a look around. The back door was open too, and by the screen door a hound wagged its tail in greeting, while the three men at the bar and the barkeep swiveled their heads and gazed blankly at the newcomer. At one of the tables four men sat playing cut-throat pinochle, and on a bench by the east wall an old-timer sat slumped with his arms folded across his chest and letting off an occasional snore.

"Mister, you want something?"

"Reason I'm in here, ain't it," Blaine McKitrick said testily. He stepped to the bar and planted a boot on the railing and tipped his hat back so they could see his chiseled gray eyes better, and at this the barkeep blinked nervously.

"We've . . . got whiskey?"

"That and some cold beer. Better bring a couple of bottles over as I brung others up here to . . . what's the name of this jerkwater place?"

"Marmouth," said the barkeep as he set two bottles on the bar, and as he did so, his vest flopped open some to reveal the town marshal's badge pinned to his faded shirt. Then he glanced frontward at Wade McKitrick and four more customers coming into his saloon. He looked back at Blaine, and mumbled, "You boys heading up to the festivities at Squaw Gap?"

"Squaw Gap—now there's a peculiar name. What is it, some Indian cantonment?" Blaine McKitrick smiled thinly.

"A town, same's Marmouth."

"Mister Marshal, this here ain't no town."

Smiling uneasily, the barkeep replied, "Big enough for us."

"You giving this gent a bad time?"

Blaine, hooking an elbow on the bar top, said, "Just want to get the lay of things hereabouts." He grabbed the stein of beer sliding to a stop in front of him, brought it to his lips and drank thirstily, and slamming the empty stein down, gestured for it to be refilled.

"Let's take that table," suggested Wade McKitrick as he turned that way and sought one of the chairs. He was a more careful drinker than his brother, but could out-drink both Blaine and Tanner in the long run. His eyes slid to Larry Madden stepping over to watch the pinochle game, then Wade turned his thoughts to Deadwood.

The seven thousand had been there, in that safety deposit box, along with further instructions. Despite this, Wade McKitrick still didn't know who was behind this plot to take out Johnston Pettigrew. Though he'd found out Pettigrew had a lot of enemies. Topping his list was still Lydel Farnsworth. Another thing had been the exchange of telegrams between Deadwood and Bozeman, territorial Montana, this chiefly to iron out a few details and tell Wade McKitrick if Pettigrew was still going to be on that train. From all the money being spent on this, there was this half-baked notion forming that just maybe more'n one man was involved. He didn't like operating in the dark, not knowing whose money he would be getting for killing Pettigrew, though McKitrick knew he'd do the job for nothing if it came down to that. There was still this bitter resentment for the way Pettigrew had set them up, and then sent lawdogs after them. They'd barely gotten out of Montana, and after splitting up, he had the misfortune to get caught at Sheridan. Once in a while he'd grimace in pain from a healing cut etched into his back by that guard's bullwhip. Then all he could think about was gunning down Johnston Pettigrew.

"Rooming houses? Yup, there's a couple of them. Downstreet a couple of blocks there's Davison's . . . and then this great big old house turned into a rooming house by Hazel Keller."

"You hear that?" said Blaine McKitrick from where he stood talking to the barkeep.

"I heard," muttered Wade as he shoved up and came over to the bar. He motioned the barkeep to the end of the bar, to add low, "This Hazel Keller a redheaded woman . . . maybe in her thirties . . ."

"She be that, awright, mister. Been here . . . by golly, goin' on three years now. You know Hazel?"

"Could be," Wade said tightly. "Could be."

"Hazel," he added nervously, "sets a fine table too, mister."

A faraway glimmer touched Wade McKitrick's eyes. It was after they'd robbed a bank down in Green River, as he recalled, that Hazel Keller had run out on him. But not before helping herself to some of that money. He figured Hazel for a

54

warm-weather gal, not someone who'd want to pine away in a place such as this. Since he was a man who didn't like to be taken advantage of, it was only fitting and proper he call upon Hazel socially. Wrangling directions from the barkeep, McKitrick strolled back to the table.

"Madden, you and Will take our hosses to that livery stable we spotted just upstreet." Then he told them how to get to the boarding house run by Hazel Keller. He led the way outside, to have Blaine fall into step with him as the others tended to the horses.

"What you fixin' to do?"

"For damned sure I ain't going courting. She owes me a free meal or two and a night's lodging."

"Expect, Wade, what she stole from you amounts to a helluva lot more." Blaine McKitrick punched a fist into his brother's arm. "Bet'cha old Hazel will pack you into her bed tonight."

"Hardly likely. Since we was fightin' like cats and dogs when old Hazel cut out on me. But for damnsure us bein' here, Blaine, will pop out a few more gray hairs."

Passing farther along a side street, and trees blocking their view, they found themselves gazing upon a rambling gabled house wearing a new coat of white paint. Out back were a shed and an outhouse and a clothesline sagging under the weight of clothes hanging from it, and some trash barrels. A light beamed out of a window on the second floor, and from a window to the right of the front door. Trees lined the walkway they went up, and when Wade McKitrick's boot hit the first porch step, a dog bounded out from under it and stood there with its hackles up and growling. Pivoting slightly, Blaine McKitrick lashed out with a boot that struck the dog alongside its jawbone. He smiled at the dog yelping back under the porch.

Without hesitating, Wade McKitrick opened the screen door and strode into the front hallway, with his boots echoing hollowly on the hardwood floor. He came to a wide open doorway just as a woman with reddish hair and handsome features appeared in it, to have fear widen Hazel Keller's eyes. A hand flew to her mouth as she said, "Wade . . . McKitrick?"

"Been a spell, Hazel." He made no attempt to remove his hat.

Now anger lifted her brows. "Don't you believe in knocking!"

"Believed in you at one time, Hazel. So just what in hell are you doing in this one-horse town?"

"Why this sudden concern about me, Wade?"

"Just surprised to see you is all, honey-bunch." He stepped closer, ran a finger along her cheekbone. "You ain't aged all that much. And still as sassy as ever."

"Wade . . . about that money . . . I . . ."

"Easy come, easy go," he said around a taut smile. "Ain't that right, Blaine?"

"Yup, the way it is."

"The truth is, Hazel, we're just passin' through. Your local saloon-owner told us about you runnin' this place. So we came over for old time's sake. There's four more, Hazel. We'll be a-needin' vittles and a place to sleep tonight. And what whiskey you've got."

"Sure . . . Wade," she muttered. "Only got five bedrooms. Two of them are rented out."

"No problem. My boys can double up."

"I'll . . . see about frying some more chicken."

"Don't forget the booze," Blaine McKitrick reminded her. He eyed her lissome figure encased in the tight-fitting dress as Hazel Keller hurried down a hallway and went into the kitchen. "Still got it, Wade. You don't sleep with old Hazel tonight, I'll take the honors."

"Sleeping with old Hazel, brother of mine, doesn't interest me right now. What does is her knowing us."

"Up here it doesn't make much difference. Come morning, Wade, we'll be long gone. They don't have a telegraph office here . . . and besides, Hazel never did have much use for the law before."

"Still, her knowing us don't set right . . . not at all, Blaine."

The kitchen was large enough to include on its hardwood floor several cabinets and two sinks, one having a pump attached to it, a four-burner kitchen stove, and ten chairs spread around the long table. There were two ceiling lamps, both throwing down light onto those seated at the table. Of the two boarders, one had come into the kitchen, seen the hardcases and done a quick turnaround, and the other simply hadn't shown.

As for Hazel Keller, there was in her a fear for what Wade McKitrick was capable of doing. His showing up had come as a complete shock. During what remained of the afternoon she'd prepared a larger supper, and when her supply of liquor had ran out, at Wade McKitrick's curt words she'd thrown on her shawl and headed over to the saloon. Right now the men seated in her kitchen were showing the effects of their drinking, especially Blaine McKitrick, as she recalled, a mean drunk.

The whiskey had also let slip out from these hardcases their intentions of heading up to Squaw Gap. What was there besides a few taverns and mercantile stores, just the one bank, and another possibility being the railroad depot. A train, maybe that was it, the McKitricks were going to hold up one of those Northern Pacific passenger trains. But all of this was none of her business. Her dread at the moment was Wade McKitrick staying at her house tonight. The money she'd taken was another worry, although it had only been around twelve hundred dollars. Surely ample pay for her granting her favors to Wade for a couple of years. But men like Wade McKitrick didn't view things that way. He was as unreliable as a norther striking out of nowhere.

"What say we head over to the saloon," said Blaine McKitrick around a couple of burps, "and stir up the locals. Maybe get in a card game."

"Too bad it didn't have a pool table."

"Well, Wade, you game for headin' over?"

"Count me in," said Wade McKitrick. "Hazel, that was mighty tasty. So much so I just might linger around here 'stead of cutting out in the morning."

After a while Hazel Keller's uninvited guests filed out of the kitchen and her boarding house. Now for her came the long chore of cleaning up. She set about this somewhat reluctantly, the anger in her simmering behind her greenish eyes at the roughhouse methods of the McKitricks and the other hardcases. When she was younger men such as this hadn't bothered her all that much, or maybe it was because she was having such fun drifting from one man to another that she hadn't taken into account just how cruel they really were. About them had been a certain hardness, in the wary way they moved and seemed to watch everything, but especially in their eyes, that with them killing was a matter-of-fact thing. This held more true for the McKitricks, she'd learned from bitter experience.

Later, after the kitchen chores were finished, Hazel Keller sat knitting in her living room, but found that she was far too nervous to do a proper job, and even a walk on the back porch didn't serve to calm her down. She'd told these men where to find their rooms, and now Hazel went to her first-floor bedroom and locked the door, made sure the window latches were in place. Then she simply turned the wick on the lamp down and stretched out on her bed without undressing. The hours dragged on, the clock on her bedstand ticking away, until shortly past one o'clock she fell asleep.

Was she dreaming or was there actually someone in her bedroom? Hazel Keller fought to come out of a restless sleep, to discover to her fear that the hand of Wade McKitrick had dropped over her mouth, and somehow the bedroom door had been pried open.

"Take it easy, Hazel," he muttered with a drunken slur.

She pulled his hand away from her mouth. "How dare you break into my bedroom."

All of a sudden Wade's eyes went ugly, and he backhanded her across the face, did it again just to make himself feel better. "You thieving bitch . . . you owe me plenty." He sort of laughed at the blood flowing out of one nostril onto her upper cheek. "As I recollect, Hazel, you was quite a package in bed."

"No, Wade, please, I . . . I have some money saved up . . . I . . ."

He fumbled out of his coat and tossed it onto a nearby chair, started unbuttoning his woolen shirt, then remembered he still had on his gunbelt. "This'll sure hamper the action in that bed of yours, Hazel. Start stripping, woman . . . or I'll rip them clothes off myself."

They pounded away from her boarding house just as the sun broke over the horizon. They left behind a ravaged woman, Hazel Keller standing halfclad in the kitchen door and too damned tired and angry to make herself presentable. But to Hazel the fact she was still alive seemed a miracle. For the drunken ramblings of the hardcases pretty much told her they were planning to kill someone up at Squaw Gap. And on the Fourth of July.

"That's about a forty mile ride up there by horseback. Longer by buggy. I've got to . . . see

60

the town marshal, Davis."

In her bedroom, Hazel Keller slipped into an old dress and fussed with her hair for a brief moment before hurrying outside. She cut through an alleyway and began angling from there across the street to the saloon, and there, cut around behind to head for a small house with a peaked roof. Her anxious pounding on the front door soon caused it to open.

"Hazel, what in tarnation . . . something wrong?"

"Those men who were here, Milo, they're heading for Squaw Gap."

"Damned good riddance."

"They plan to kill someone."

"Now, Hazel, you can't be sure about that . . ."

"Dammit, Milo, they were drunk . . . bragged on what they were gonna do."

"I don't know about . . ."

"Dammit, they're the McKitricks! Not just some half-hearted rustlers. Someone's got to head up there, Milo, warn them."

"Doggonit, Hazel, I've got a business to run."

"Isn't someone's life more important than selling rotgut? You've got to go up there, to Squaw Gap, Milo. The killing's gonna happen tomorrow, on the Fourth. Well?"

"I see you've got a black eye, Hazel, some bruises. Them gents treated you awful mean. But going to Squaw Gap, all I've got is your words on this. Just don't make no sense."

"Stay here then, Milo Davis, I'll go. I'm borrowing your horse. You . . . you . . ." Clamping her teeth together, Hazel Keller spun around and hur-

61

ried away, to throw back, "You damned skinflint!"

"You owe me, Blaine."

"Figured it wouldn't be her, but the town marshal."

About a half-day's riding had brought the McKitricks northward on a trail weaving alongside the Little Missouri River. Some time ago Larry Madden, who'd been hanging back, had cantered up to tell the others a rider was pounding in on their backtrail. They had pulled away from the river road and brought their horses onto an escarpment giving them a wide view of both the river and its approaches.

Squinting distastefully at an approaching scattering of cloud, Brent Wilmar spat out, "Guess we'll be needing our slickers."

"Just a passing shower, Will."

"Maybe so, but this shirt I bought back at Deadwood ain't about to get a drop of rainwater on it. Wade, you fixing to take her out?"

"He ain't," snickered Madden, "gonna invite her along."

When Hazel Keller had brought her loping horse around still another bend in the road, and was about a quarter of a mile away, Wade McKitrick unlimbered his Winchester as he kneed his bronc off the elevation. At its base, he cantered toward the road and drew up to bring the rifle to his right shoulder. He sighted in on the horse and squeezed off a shot, the sharp report scaring up game birds and dropping the woman out of the saddle. The horse staggered and tried to rear up, and then just flopped down. Now he loped toward Hazel Keller making a desperate run for sheltering rocks, but putting away his rifle and drawing one of his Peacemakers. A casual bullet nipped one of her churning boot heels away, and tumbling her to the ground.

In her hand there was a sixgun, and Hazel Keller triggered the weapon to have the bullet miss by a wide margin. Wade McKitrick simply smiled and came in closer, and he said chidingly, "Told you you still owe me, Hazel."

"Why . . . why did you have to show up, damn you?"

"A small world. Told you, Hazel, nobody steals from me . . . not even some old slut."

Desperately she brought up her weapon as he fired, the leaden slug punching into her chest, another, and he smiled that tight smile of his when she toppled backward, knowing that Hazel Keller was dead, smug in the knowledge that she'd paid him back.

"Now on to Squaw Gap and some more killings."

Chapter Six

Depot Agent Clyde Dexter came out onto the platform and laid watchful eyes upon a freight train rattling westward. It was around mid-morning, the passenger train from Bismarck having already passed through. A few passengers had gotten off, some here for tomorrow's big Fourth of July celebration, and a couple of locals. The sky had a brassy blue tint to it, and he said somewhat sagely, "It's gonna be another scorcher."

Unlike other depot agents, Dexter preferred wearing suits and a derby, this being replaced by a more westerny hat some time ago. The sultry heat had caused him to peel out of his suit coat. He was a wispy man at around five seven. But possessed of steady brown eyes and a deep baritone voice which carried the ring of authority. Sundays he sang in the choir over at St. Thomas Evangelical Church.

Somewhat reluctantly he had allowed bunting to be strung up on the depot. Before on the Fourth the townspeople of Squaw Gap hadn't considered the depot to be of much importance. Johnston Pettigrew coming here on a Northern Pacific train had changed all of that, and now Dexter shot a displeasing glance up at the big white banner welcoming this Montana politician to Squaw Gap.

Something of this nature should be reserved for only two people, both presidents, one of this country, the other of the Northern Pacific Railroad.

Just past the empty baggage cart he gazed upon a trio of loafers taking their ease on one of the benches, and he swung that way and said, "Orville, I expect you could whittle someplace else."

"I know where the broom is, Clyde. You getting worked up about all of this?"

"About this Pettigrew coming here. As long as it brings in revenue for the railroad it has my blessings, I suppose. Have you seen the Oberlander boy, Marcus?"

"Yup," said another, "idling over by Olivetti's."

Dexter glanced down at the telegram that had come in about an hour ago and mumbled, "Should have been here by now. Usually is on time."

"I could deliver it, Clyde, say for six bits."

"No bother, Riley, as the boy is about here."

When he saw the depot agent standing out on the platform, Marcus Oberlander broke into a shambling run. He was exactly a month past his thirteenth birthday, splintery of build, with a spattering of freckles covering his face. He had long arms and inquiring blue eyes. He wore blue coveralls, the blue shirt with the sleeves rolled up past his elbows and an old cowboy's hat that pressed against the tops of his outthrust ears. Marcus wore his last birthday present, bullhide cowboy boots into which he'd tucked the bottoms of his coveralls.

"Tardiness is not a virtue, Marcus," scolded Dexter.

"Yeah, I know. Guess I should talk my pa into buying me a watch."

"This telegram is for that traveling preacher. Make sure he gets it. Then don't wander off someplace but come straight back here. I want you to sweep the platform . . . and perhaps clean out that back storeroom."

"Right away, Mr. Dexter." With the yellow envelope in one hand, Marcus spun away to trot along the tracks before cutting toward the road.

That he was carrying a telegram meant for Thaddeus Beecher added more excitement to a day already filled with other promising adventures. Right away he discounted the dance that was to be held at Moseby's Dance Emporium, for closer at hand was the small circus being set up on a meadow fringing onto Horse Head Creek. He'd seen the one elephant and monkeys in cages, and in his mind a killer lion in that big iron cage, where actually the animal was pacing about its cage on aging legs and was tamer than most broncs hereabouts. But the greatest excitement for Marcus Oberlander were the firecrackers bulging out a back pocket, and here on Barcome Street, his view, as he scuffled along, of the bunting strung across the wide thoroughfare and the people crowding the boardwalks where some merchants had brought their wares outside.

He drew up sharply, held there, as a bunch of waddies suddenly swung their horses out of a side street and went boldly past him, and with his eyes taking in the 777 brand on the horses. He knew one of them, Skeeter Burns, but the waddy was too busy taking in the swinging batwings at the Western Bar to notice some gawking yonker.

Remembering the telegram, and the promise of seeing the preacher, Marcus Oberlander swerved around a fat lady glaring after him and tramped across the boardwalk to dash into the lobby of the Starbuck Hotel, where the desk clerk yelled at the door slamming shut.

"How many times, Oberlander, do I have to tell you not to come busting in here."

"But I've got . . ."

At that moment Thaddeus Beecher called out from where he was coming down the staircase, "Easy on the boy."

"This here telegram's for you, Reverend Beecher." He was in awe of tall and dark-bearded Reverend Thaddeus Beecher. And from close observation knew that an occasional swear word passed through Beecher's lips, had once glimpsed the preacher sneaking a bottle of whiskey up to his hotel room, and that Beecher carried a handgun, along with the ever-present Bible. He would be sorry when the preacher left, as this was what he'd mentioned to Marcus in a casual aside one day. Lastly, he felt Thaddeus Beecher had more of the earmarks of a gunhand than a man packing religious words.

"A telegram?" Thaddeus Beecher dug out a silvery dime. "Here, Marcus, I do thank, you."

"Yessir, Reverend Beecher," beamed the yonker as he spun to head at a trot toward the lobby door, this bringing a painful grimace from the desk clerk.

The man known hereabouts as Thaddeus Beecher could feel the curious eyes of the desk clerk upon him as he tore open the envelope. He'd stepped closer to a window and turned so that his back was to the clerk, for worry had settled in his eyes. Only his brothers were supposed to know he was here at Squaw Gap. Now the telegram, he found, had come from Bozeman, and bore no name to tell him who'd sent it. There was a brief message: Pettigrew will arrive there on North Coast Limited.

"So he'll be here," muttered Tanner McKitrick. "Just hope my brothers make it." He folded the telegram and thrust it into a coat pocket.

As his habit had been since coming here, Tanner McKitrick left the hotel and trudged downstreet to find a booth in Ma Schwartz's Corner Cafe. The food, he'd discovered, was better than at the Claremont Hotel and a greasy spoon cafe at the eastern end of Barcome Street. One of his capabilities was of eating heartily in spite of worry or if a lawman knew a McKitrick was in his bailiwick. Coffee, thick with chicory, was brought to him in a big cup by one of the two waitresses, who took his customary order of steak and eggs and hash browns and went away, to leave Tanner McKitrick sipping thoughtfully.

Apparently, he surmised, there'd been correspondence of some kind between Deadwood and Bozeman. This would explain that telegram finding him here at Squaw Gap in his role as Thaddeus Beecher. Too bad that what they were fixing to do tomorrow involved gunplay. For Squaw Gap had

68

proved to be a cowtown where a man could hole up when things got hairy at other places. That night with Dalphine Wickland had also served to take away some of Tanner McKitrick's uneasy edges. Later tonight his intentions were to sneak back over there and have another go-around with the woman. There were a lot of women in other places who'd had a taste of his charms, and maybe he'd sired a kid or two. This was something McKitrick had never stuck around long enough to find out.

The cafe had folks traipsing in or leaving, and Tanner McKitrick was halfway through his t-bone still taking up most of his plate when a familiar voice brought his eyebrows up, to have him look at one of his brothers easing into the booth.

"Figured I'd find you at a place like this chowing down," Wade McKitrick said quietly. "Or at some saloon."

"Men spouting holy words don't hit for them places, brother Wade."

"Or at some cathouse."

"A tempting idea," said Tanner McKitrick around a growing smile. "Next time you're gonna pack a Bible and spout hellfire and brimstone words, Wade, as this is wearing me down."

"One more day."

He took the telegram out of his pocket and let it flutter onto the table top. "Arrived this morning."

"Just wanted to make sure Pettigrew would be on that train."

"Whose money is behind this?"

"Got my thoughts on that, Tanner. Don't rightly

know we'll find that out until we head into Montana. But I've a hunch it's a woman."

"And not . . . Lydel Farnsworth—"

"Could be Farnsworth's wife. Just before we gun Pettigrew down we're to give him a little message."

"Such as?"

"Beware the thorns of a red, red rose."

"Don't make no sense, Wade, a red rose?"

"Got to be a woman, maybe Farnsworth's wife, who's bankrolling this. That steak any good?"

"Better'n most."

"I figure come tomorrow we'll be too busy trying to kill Pettigrew to deliver any personal messages. Let him die wondering who set him up."

"The way I feel about it. We'll take him out just upstreet at that platform."

"Why not on the train?"

"Once we gun him down, folks here will get a posse together and be hot on our trail. What we need is something to slow them down." Tanner McKitrick let his fork and knife clatter onto his plate as he rose and left some money to pay for his meal.

"Just what do you have in mind?"

Outside the cafe, Tanner McKitrick, a toothpick floating in one corner of his mouth, said, "Where's Blaine and any others you brought along?"

"Camped out south of here by a creek. Figured I'd have them drift in later in the day . . . and separately. Now I'm fixing to buy some whiskey and food and head out there. You never did answer my question, Tanner?"

"They'll be on the speaker's platform around one

. . . Pettigrew and some other hotwinders. When Pettigrew gets to farting some patriotic words, we come riding in . . . from both ends of the street . . . sort of easylike. We get Pettigrew first. Then, Wade, we turn our guns on some locals ̄as we break out of here . . . a woman or two . . . or whoever gets in our gunsights."

"Makes sense," grinned Wade McKitrick. "You coming out to our camp?"

"Better not, Wade. We'll get together after sundown, up in my room at the Starbuck Hotel. Iron out a few details. And speaking of tomorrow, after Pettigrew's train arrives we'd best keep off the streets. He spots a McKitrick, well, the game's over."

"Until tonight, then. Take care. By the way, Tanner, knowing you, there was a local belle or two that fell for your line of bull."

"Was one," he admitted. "Plan to keep her warm later tonight. Now ease out of here, Wade. And damned glad to see you again."

Chapter Seven

Tying his horse to the buggy frame, Rain Lonigan moved over to help his wife down. Once they got settled in at the Claremont Hotel, Jillian would head over to see Doc Barcome, and with Rain Lonigan checking in with his deputy, young Dave Jamison.

Waiting until those he worked for and their children were in the hotel, Casey Tessler reined the gelding downstreet. Tessler didn't cotton to coming into town all that often, would have preferred staying out at the Rocking L instead of partaking in these patriotic festivities. But Rain had kept insisting he needed a break from the ranch. Casey Tessler was the kind of man people liked having around. He had a grudging but not mean kind of humor, and would hang out at one of the saloons though he drank sparingly. A few who knew him waved casually as Casey Tessler swung off Barcome Street and eased the buggy along the side wall of Gintley's Livery Stable. Working the chaw of tobacco bulging out one cheek, he gimpied out of the buggy seat and began unhooking the gelding from the wagon traces. After both horses were stabled, he spent a few minutes gabbing with Ezra Gintley, one of the first to settle in here at Squaw Gap.

Then Casey Tessler felt the hunger pangs as he began that short walk back to Barcome Street. Almost there, he took the time to stop and eyeball some youngsters darting past him and south along the side street, and looking farther to the south, Tessler spotted a couple of striped circus tents before he heard that elephant cutting loose.

"What in tarnation? Celebrations. Then this big dance tonight. Just an excuse for some to unlimber their fists. Well, since I'm here might's well take advantage of a few things."

On the boardwalk, he weaved slowly past merchandise set out on tables or in barrels and others like him taking in the sights. What he needed was a couple of work shirts, and more importantly, new red flannels. He came upon the shirts hanging from a clothes rack out in front of The Republican Mercantile Store. As he stood there pondering over buying the shirts, his eyes chanced to gaze into the wide display window, to see reflecting there two men just emerging from the Corner Cafe.

"There's that preacher . . . what's his name, Beecher. And chatting with some hardcase? Know I've seen him before, and maybe the other one. But where, Colorado, Wyoming? But it'll come; maybe after I have some vittles."

Among the morning mail Rain Lonigan found a couple of wanted posters. He glanced at them, with his deputy, Davey Jamison, looking over Rain's shoulder. "Some outlaw named Wade McKitrick busted out of the Wyoming territorial

73

prison. A mean looking dude."

"Arty Greenway just shoves them in that drawer over there. Come winter he uses them to kindle a fire. A waste of time sending them here."

"What about tonight, Davey, you pairing up with Sidwell?"

"You're ramrodding things, Rain. Suits me. Shouldn't have too much trouble over at that dance. It's the saloons I'm worried about."

"And these kids with their firecrackers. Caused the mayor's horse to stampede just as he got settled in the saddle. Couldn't help laughing at what happened."

"Yup, Weaver flopping out of the saddle like that and tearing up his shoulder."

"Could have been worse," said Rain Lonigan. "Trouble is, those kids setting those firecrackers and rockets off at night, someone might take it for a gun. But ... the city council okayed the merchants selling this stuff. Me, just be glad when Marshal Greenway takes over again."

"Guess I'll go home then, Rain. Sure you don't need me?"

"No, take a break, Davey. This is gonna be one long weekend."

Squaw Gap was a typical cowtown in that it had more saloons and gaming dens than places to worship. Sometimes railroad section crews would overnight or stay here for a few days, and to avail themselves of the bars and other business places. Too, it was a place popular with ranchers and cowhands, since Marshal Greenway didn't interfere all that much when these men were in town. Once in a while hard-eyed men would pass through, and then drift on. Perhaps, mused Rain Lonigan, as he shouldered into a saloon, these hardcases were looking for more action.

"Howdy . . . Lonigan, is it?"

"Yup, Reverend Beecher, Lonigan will do." He glanced at the bottle of sasparilla Thaddeus Beecher had at his elbow. And beyond Beecher at the editor of the *Squaw Gap Chronicle*.

"I invited him in for a drink," explained Earl Paulson, before whom on the bar stood a bottle of Four Roses whiskey and an empty shot glass. "I even insisted the good preacher partake of the devil's brew."

"Once upon a time I did enjoy drinking with the devil, gentlemen, but having seen the light, besides suffering from a kidney condition, no longer do I indulge."

"A pity," said the editor. "Reverend Beecher tells me he'll be leaving us shortly."

"Yes, though I've grown quite fond of your town, there's this urge to strike east. I hear Medora is a place that needs salvation."

"Can get rough at times over there."

"Well, gentlemen, I shall take my leave. Obliged for the drink, Mr. Paulson. Perhaps I'll see you in church on Sunday . . ."

In response Earl Paulson refilled his shot glass, and after Thaddeus Beecher had left, he turned serious eyes upon Rain Lonigan. "What do you make of him?"

"Beecher? Maybe just a panhandler working this town until we tire of him. You ever hear him preach?"

"My wife, God bless her, takes care of that

chore in our family. Yes, yes, I should go to church more. Just maybe, Rain, I've gotten old . . . and downright cynical. The newspaper game will do that to a man. Marshal, do you ever get bad feelings about a man? Beecher, here, gets under my skin, somehow."

"They say men of the Lord work in mysterious ways."

"That's just it, Lonigan. Something tells me Thaddeus Beecher is no preacher."

"Maybe a lawyer taking it on the lam."

"Or a newspaperman," laughed Paulson. He gestured with his empty shot glass. "It's what I see in his eyes, Lonigan, that troubles me. Behind all that smooth biblical talk and piety is a man been a lot of hard places. Behind those pious eyes lurks the true Thaddeus Beecher, if indeed, that is his truthful name."

"Funny," said Rain Lonigan, "that you should feel the same way."

"So, Lonigan, I'm not the only one."

"Not me, but Casey Tessler. Casey mentioned it just the other day that he's almost certain he's seen Beecher before. But if he's leaving, so much the better, I suppose."

"And I'm heading back to my office," said Earl Paulson. "Got to write up more lies about the esteemed Johnston Pettigrew. Tell everyone what a great man Pettigrew is . . . malarky like that."

After making his rounds, which included the business section, and a jaunt down to check over what was going on at the circus, Rain Lonigan went back to the Claremont Hotel, to be greeted up in their rooms by his children, and where he said anxiously to his wife, Jillian, "What did the doctor say?"

"That everything's fine. I can even go to the dance tonight . . . but no fast stuff, Mr. Lonigan."

"Daddy, I'm hungry."

"Guess we all are," said Rain. "Want to eat here at the hotel?"

"Some church women are serving dinner at the social club."

"Yes, just so you can go over there and catch up on the latest gossip." He smiled into Jillian's eyes before kissing her lightly. Being the wife of a rancher had denied her the opportunity to build up a lot of friendships, and sometimes it was Rain's notion they should move into town. He'd heard the railroad was hiring, among other places. But to give up something that had always been a part of his life would be hard. Cattle and ranching were all he'd known, and to leave it, Rain felt, would make him a lesser man somehow. Jillian wasn't one to complain, and she was the daughter of a rancher. Still, there were times when he could see that lonely glimmer in her eyes.

Out on the street, Rain Lonigan gazed with some concern at three men riding by on horses bearing brands unknown to him. They had the look of hardcases. Maybe they'd drifted over from Medora, or in from Montana. But in any case, he should expect that a lot of strangers would be here for the celebration. Quietly he muttered, "Wearing this badge can sure turn a man into a worrywart. Maybe they're just cowpokes."

"What's that, dear?"

Around a rueful grin he said, "Just ruminating to myself."

"Daddy, can we go over to the circus."

"Chowtime first, Sara."

"Oh, daddy, I'm not hungry."

"You'll eat," he said more sharply than he intended, "and afterward you and Kiley can go to the circus."

"Do I have to babysit Kiley again?"

Kiley Lonigan glared at his sister and said, "I'm big enough to take care of myself."

"Hush now," broke in Jillian, "your father's got enough on his mind. We'll eat first. Then, Sara, you take your brother with you."

When they were inside the Squaw Gap Social Club, Jillian Lonigan overruled her husband's decision that she find a seat at one of the tables while he went through the serving line. "Heavens, Rain, I can manage."

"Well, Jillian," said Dalphine Wickland as she strode by, "long time no see."

"Ranch work is never done."

"When is the baby due?"

"In October. I'm hoping the baby is born on Rain's birthday." Jillian Lonigan frowned. "You seem awful sunshiny, Dalphine. Are you seeing . . . someone?"

"Yes, I am," she replied quickly as a blush reddened her cheeks. "I'd better get to collecting plates and silverware so others can sit down."

"She does seem awful chipper," commented Rain.

"About time Dalphine took an interest in

things."

"Just who can she be seeing?"

"Does it matter? And besides, Rain, that's none of our business."

"Suppose not." Now he trailed after his wife and children taking their plates of food over to a table. Seated farther along the tables butted together were Mayor Armond Weaver and a couple of businessmen. He nodded at them.

"Rain, I want to see you after you're done eating," said the mayor. "It's about letting the saloons stay open past the normal closing time. Just for this weekend. Got to make hay while the sun shines."

"Making hay as you call it, Mr. Weaver, means we'll have to put on extra deputies." Even as he spoke, Rain Lonigan knew he'd be working longer hours this weekend for the same pay, and the thought kind of rankled him, so that he stopped eating for a moment. It was simply that Squaw Gap couldn't afford to hire more deputies.

"I'll understand, dear, if you can't take me to the dance tonight."

"Jillian, by rights I should hand in my badge," he said softly. "No, somehow I'll find time to sweep you out onto the dance floor."

"Despite my very obvious condition," she teased.

"Yup, despite that."

Chapter Eight

Another Northern Pacific train had passed through around dusk, but not before a couple of dozen people from Dickinson and points farther east had gotten off to become a part of the Squaw Gap festivities. There were no vacancies at the rooming houses and hotels, and quite a few townsfolks had taken people into their homes. Some cowhands from the Ox Bow spread had pitched a tent west along the creek, their campfire a tiny ember of light behind a copse of trees. The circus was also marked by lantern lights as a steady throng strolled to it on dusky sidestreets. Downtown, there was activity from one end of Barcome Street to the other, a jostling and boisterous crowd that stuck more to the wide street than the boardwalks, this because only those on foot were allowed access to it, with buggies and wagons and other vehicular traffic forced to proceed along other streets.

For Rain Lonigan and his deputies it was proving to be about as much as they could handle. Whenever Rain heard firecrackers rat-tat-tatting in alleyways or on the streets, an anxious hand would touch the curving handle of his Smith & Wesson. About an hour or so before sundown the town band had set to with hearty renditions of patriotic songs; they'd broken up a few minutes ago. Once a runaway horse had broken away from a hitching post, its flight caused by a yonker setting off some firecrackers, and sped crazily along Barcome Street until a mounted cowhand had taken off after it, to the cheers of most. There'd been a few fights, in some of the bars, and one at a gaming casino over one of J.D. Richard's bar girls. But much to Rain Lonigan's easing of mind, no gunplay. It had been suggested that everyone check their guns at the marshal's office. This proposal had been vehemently opposed by most of the ranchers.

Around seven o'clock he'd come across Casey Tessler playing checkers with an old crony over at the Square Deal Saloon. They'd exchanged pleasantries, with Rain turning down Casey's offer of a drink. For some unexplained reason Casey Tessler had brought up the worrying subject, as he'd called it, of Reverend Thaddeus Beecher.

"You seen Beecher around tonight, Rain?"

"Can't recollect that I have. Yup, come to think of it, I did . . . saw Beecher strolling into the Claremont Hotel."

"Come on, Casey, quit nagging on about that sky pilot and get to moving them checkers," scolded his opponent. "Never seen you play so bad."

"Well, Oliver, a beer says I beat you this game."

"Hell, Casey, you owe me five beers now."

"Double or nothing?"

With an amused grin splitting his lips, Rain Lonigan had left the saloon to continue on with his duties as town marshal. In another saloon, Jake's Old Tyme Tavern, he couldn't help noticing the presence of two hard-eyed drifters playing a game of eight ball. But they were playing quietly, while another drifter sat with his legs crossed and a stein of beer at his elbow as he watched the pool game. All three wore their guns low, threw guarded looks Rain Lonigan's way as he came back.

Rain allowed a tight smile to show. "You boys passing through or here for the weekend?"

"Any law against celebrating the Fourth here . . . or any other place?"

"Reckon not. Where are you boys from?"

Larry Madden spoke up from where he was sitting at the table. "Just some drifting cowpokes, marshal. We heard the 777 spread is hiring."

"Appears they are," replied Rain Lonigan. "Well, don't get too boisterous." He ambled away.

Jesse Cairne, a sneer lifting one corner of his wide mouth, turned to Madden and said, "Squaw Gap don't have much in the way of law."

"Keep it cool," Madden warned him.

The other player, Smithly, picked up a cube of blue chalk. "Yeah, Cairne, 'cause we'll be out of this place tomorrow."

"Just funning is all," fumed the hardcase. "Hell, I'll buy the next round."

* * *

"Looky here now, Kiley, an' Sara, don't you be a-telling your pa I've been springin' for sasparilla and such." He handed the offspring of Rain Lonigan a dime apiece and watched them dart across the dance floor.

Casey Tessler and a couple of others were standing in the front hallway, and the benches along the wall were occupied. At the back end of the large hall two fiddlers and a banjo player cued in to the opening notes of a whitehaired gent seated before the piano, then to the tunes of a sprightly waltz the dance floor became crowded. Tessler smiled at Rain Lonigan dancing with his wife, and he remarked, "Was quite a dancer in my day."

"That being some time ago, Casey."

He snorted, "Not that long ago. I ain't no Ancient Mariner . . . nor stoved up with rheumatism like you, Al." About a half-hour ago Tessler had gotten tired of that checker game, and for a change of pace decided to amble over here. What caught a displeased eye was the sight of Thaddeus Beecher coming in a side door. The preacher was beginning to be a burr under Casey Tessler's saddle blanket, but try as he might Tessler still couldn't recall where it was he'd seen Beecher before. But wherever it was, came Casey's notion, it was connected with violence somehow.

"Al, you've been places."

"Some I want to forget about. Yup, I see you've set your eyes on that sky pilot again. It's sure eating at you, Casey, you not remembering where you crossed trails before."

"I always thought it was the legs that went first."

"Your condition, Casey, was probably brought on by drinking too much beer over at the Square Deal. Come on, let's mosey over to some saloon and lie about what we used to do once."

"Knowing you, Al, I feel a heap of white lies coming on. But at least we can roll dice to see who buys." Casey Tessler set his hat lower over his eyes as he took a final survey of the dance floor. Out there he could see Dalphine Wickland doing some fancy steps with Thaddeus Beecher, and as Tessler started to swing around, out of the corner of his eye he chanced to notice a tall, dark man motioning the preacher toward a side door. Tessler held there, with his eyes squinting thoughtfully, and then he added, "Al, I'll join you over at the Square Deal in a couple of minutes."

"Sure . . . Casey?" But he'd said it to Casey Tessler fringing along the dance floor and going out the side door.

It took a moment for Casey Tessler to locate the man who'd drawn him outside, and now he set out after Thaddeus Beecher and the stranger, finding the alley behind Barcome Street. As he entered the mouth of the alley, a cat darting out brought Tessler up short, to have him choke off a cuss word. Midway up the alley he could make out the familiar form of Thaddeus Beecher veer over and open the back door of the Starbuck Hotel, and then both men went inside. Picking up his gait, Casey Tessler brushed around an empty barrel, and then eased up to the open doorway when he spotted the men he was trailing standing in the back hallway. Easing up closer, he heard the man claiming to be Thaddeus Beecher say, "I tell you, Wade, it'll be better to take out Pettigrew when he's on that speaker's platform and not by the train."

"Could be you're right, Tanner, but I don't know . . . just feel uneasy about this."

"What's the difference where we kill that damned politician."

"Look brother Tanner, don't be getting your dander up. You figure us taking out some others will help us get away . . . so be it."

Outside, Casey Tessler sucked night air into his mouth and drew it inside nervously. Springing away from the dark edges of his memory came a name renowned where outlaws rode: Tanner McKitrick. The one with him, as he recalled now, was another McKitrick, Wade. Where had he run into them? Yup, southwesterly in Colorado, and at Arriba on the north fork of the Republican River. It had been just another peaceful cowtown such as Squaw Gap when the McKitricks arrived. Not on the stagecoach or train or peacefullike but pouring out sudden death after holding up the only bank. The one lawman had been killed outright and a few foolish enough to exchange gunfire. During all of this Casey Tessler had etched into his mind, forever he thought, the sadistic face of Tanner McKitrick, unbearded at the time and a lot younger.

"And they plan to kill a lot of innocent

people," muttered Casey Tessler as he reached a shaking hand for his double-action Trantor. The five-shot revolver grasped in his right hand, he took the one step that carried him into the halo of dim light coming from farther up and ghosting back along the hallway. "Gents, one quick move and I start pouring lead into your mangy hides. 'Cause I remember you, Tanner McKitrick, down in Colorado it was . . . at Arriba."

At the unexpected appearance of Casey Tessler, both men had swung that way, by habit to have a hand snake toward their weapons. It was Tanner McKitrick who spoke first and around a smile framed amidst his thick black-graying beard, "Friend, you startled us. I was just giving some spiritual words of encouragement to a Christian brother of mine."

"None of you damned McKitricks are Christians. And that Bible you're toting, Tanner McKitrick, is pure blasphemy. That's it . . . elevate them hands away from them weapons . . . easy, easy. He's a brother all right, Wade, I reckon. And a killer same's you."

A surprised expression widened Casey Tessler's eyes as something hard thudded into his back. Too late he remembered there was a third McKitrick brother. For a moment he held there, impaled by a hunting knife, shock flaring wider his eyes, now both body and weapon sagging downward, and coughing blood, he died.

Blaine McKitrick appeared. "I get tired of baby-sitting you two."

Wade McKitrick laughed.

86

A wary-eyed Tanner McKitrick said, "It was bound to happen . . . someone recognizing us." He cast a nervous glance up the hallway. Now back to his brothers. "His body . . . take it out by the creek. Make it look like you're three drunken cowhands looking for a quiet place to do some more drinking." He picked up Tessler's hat, and the handgun, and thrust the hat at Blaine. "After you get rid of the body, round up the others and head back to your camp."

Blaine McKitrick flared out with, "The night's too damned young."

Wade said, "Tanner's right. We could be recognized what with all these people pouring in for the weekend. Anyway, tomorrow we'll be heading out of here."

After his brothers had hoisted the body up and were gone, Tanner McKitrick closed the back door and stepped out into the alleyway. He held in the shadows for a moment. It was bound to happen, he mused, someone recognizing the McKitricks. But despite this, there was an easing of tension. For all Squaw Gap had for law was a parttime town marshal and a handful of deputies more used to punching cattle or loafing. He'd also had the notion only those too lazy to work or too nervous to steal turned to wearing badges. As for tomorrow, they still had the element of surprise on their side. While tonight Tanner McKitrick, and as he retraced his path back toward Moseby's Dance Emporium, smiled when he thought about that widow woman, Dalphine Wickland. For certain she had a big cleavage and a bigger lust for him. To mind came a passage from the New Testament.

"How'd it go—yup, bringing in the sheep. But for this unsavory sky pilot just one ewe will do."

Chapter Nine

Just before daybreak someone with no respect for those still trying to sleep began clanging the bell over at St. Thomas Evangelical Church, this, and with others setting off strings of firecrackers.

By habit an early riser, Rain Lonigan cast a wry grin in the direction of the church just before entering a downtown cafe, where he found a booth already occupied by Doc D.B. Barcome. Rain, after allowing a waitress to fill his coffee cup, said, "You been celebrating all night, doc?"

"Wish it was that, Rain. Nope, was called out to Emery Nelson's place; missus had another stroke."

"Sorry to hear that." Stirring sugar around in his cup, Rain added, "You didn't happen to see Casey Tessler around last night?"

"Early on I did. Could be he headed back to the ranch—"

"Not at night Casey wouldn't. But I expect he'll turn up sometime this morning. Never seen Squaw Gap so crowded before."

"I figure more will be coming in on the trains . . . and some more from the ranches. By the way, I checked on Arty Greenway yesterday—expect to hand that badge back next week."

"About time," said Rain Lonigan. Though another smile appeared, there was still in Rain's eyes a worried glimmer. Along with his concern about the missing Casey Tessler, last night while checking around town he'd spotted three hardcases reining their broncs away from Gintley's Livery Stable, and by the uncertain glow of a street light Rain could almost swear one of them had his face adorning one of the wanted posters in the marshal's office. Shortly afterward Rain had gone over to the town jail to leaf through the few readers. Sure enough, there it had been, a reader telling him that Brent "Will" Wilmar was wanted for an assortment of heinous crimes in Montana and Wyoming, and further, that Wilmar was known to associate with the McKitrick brothers. He couldn't find any readers on the McKitricks, and at the time supposed this was because Arty Greenway had thrown them away.

Now, plunking down coin to pay for his light breakfast of bacon and eggs, acting town marshal Rain Lonigan left the cafe and headed upstreet for the Claremont Hotel. At the moment Rain was the only lawman on duty, but around nine this morning his deputies would show. Just as Rain came to a street corner, the mayor of Squaw Gap appeared, with an arm lifting to take in the banners strung across the street.

"Cost us a lot of money, marshal. But it isn't too often we get in a famous politician."

"I just hope Johnston Pettigrew lives up to his billing."

"He will, Lonigan, you can be assured about that. And did you find out who rang the church bell? Intolerable, I'd say."

"Just some kids, I reckon. I'll take a ringing church bell over those firecrackers, Mayor Weaver. I was hoping the merchants wouldn't sell fireworks this year. Caused one horse to stampede. Just pure luck nobody got hurt."

"Now, Lonigan, without fireworks it wouldn't be much of a Fourth," the mayor chided.

Then the mayor waddled on before Rain Lonigan could ask if he'd seen Casey Tessler during last night's festivities. And Rain muttered, "Doggone firecrackers. Anything to make a profit for the merchants." Crossing the narrow gap of a side street between the buildings, he stepped up onto the boardwalk while setting a squinting eye upon the sun just beginning to rim over the horizon. Despite the few shadows still embracing Squaw Gap, the stirring wind carried with it a metallic heat. Yesterday it had been in the low eighties; it would be hotter today, and windier. Meaning the saloons and gaming casinos would sell a lot of whiskey and beer, which to Rain meant there'd be fisticuffs and maybe gunplay.

Striding into the lobby of the Claremont Hotel, he stopped at the check-in counter and swung the register book around. Some of the names were familiar, and then the clerk appeared holding a cup of coffee and a plate on which there reposed a beef sandwich. "Jonesy, give me a rundown on some of these names. Perkins, here, what about him?"

"Heck, marshal, Perkins has been passing through here for years. Sells a line of women's garments, underpinnings and such. Any particular name you're looking for?"

"I'm looking for those wearing the stamp of gunhand."

"Some cowhands checked in, Rain, a couple of plainsmen—other than that folks we know. You expecting trouble?"

"Don't know, Jonesy," Rain Lonigan murmured, and tugging his Stetson lower over his forehead. "Seen Casey around?"

"Over to Moseby's . . . that being last night. Yup . . . seems to me Casey left kind of hurriedly." A grin etched itself across the wizened face of the clerk. "Could be he went sparking some bar girl."

"Could be," Rain said but without much conviction, and flicking a finger to the brim of his hat, he left.

Though it was only around seven, the wide reaches of Barcome Street were being spanned by those coming out of the hotels and boarding houses in search of a morning meal. A few surreys and buggies had appeared, but on side streets to tie up there, and some saddled horses. In passing along the boardwalk on his way toward the Starbuck Hotel, Rain noted to his displeasure that a few saloons were throwing out lamplight. Through the front windows he caught glimpses of a few early risers elbowed up at bars.

"Got to have galvanized stomachs," was Rain's silent comment as he broke stride and veered closer to a building. He set his pondering eyes upon Thaddeus Beecher just exiting from the Starbuck Hotel. Perhaps it was the way Casey Tessler had rambled on about the preacher that had given Rain pause, this at the moment to arouse in him unkind feelings of his own. Casey, he knew, was never a man to talk unkindly about anyone. But during a lifetime spanning nearly sixty years he realized that Casey Tessler had seen more places than most. Perhaps, as voiced by Tessler, this Beecher was a bogus man of the bible, an outlaw, maybe.

"Packing this badge is wearing me out." Saying this, he went on as Thaddeus Beecher came down off the boardwalk and began angling across the street toward a cafe.

In the lobby of the Starbuck Hotel, Marshal Rain Lonigan had to wait as the desk clerk tried to tell an older couple all of the rooms were taken, and with the clerk saying, "I'm sorry, Mr. Burnside, we simply did not get your letter requesting a room for this weekend."

"I mailed it out of Bismarck nearly a month ago, dammit. I tell you I demand a room."

"Perhaps I can help," cut in Rain Lonigan.

"Well, marshal, perhaps you can," said the angry Mr. Burnside from Bismarck, territorial Dakota.

"No sense taking what happened out on the night clerk. Rooms are full up . . . but friends of ours have this big house up on Cedar Street . . . got an empty bedroom or two."

In a demure aside to her husband the woman

93

murmured, "Really, Jaspar, why don't we catch the next train for Bismarck."

"No, we came to have a little fun. I appreciate the offer, marshal . . ."

"Rain Lonigan. I'll be with you soon as I have a private word with the desk clerk." He stepped past the Burnsides moving toward the lobby door. "Mike, did a man named Wilmar check in here?"

"Nope."

"Or maybe some friends of that preacher, Thaddeus Beecher . . ."

"Funny thing about that, marshal," said the clerk as he scratched at his thinning hairline. "Beecher did have a couple of visitors; night before last. Strangers. Hazarding a guess, I'd say they were gamblers . . . or men riding on the fringes of the law. Then, marshal"—the desk clerk nodded toward a back hallway—"appeared to have been a little ruckus back there . . . that being last night. At the time I was busy checking in some guests. Went back later . . . some twenty minutes or so . . . you know, to check it out. Well, marshal, didn't find anybody back there. But on the floor there was some fresh blood."

"A hideout gun wouldn't make too much noise," Rain speculated.

"Didn't hear any shot. A knife, maybe."

"Not much to go on. You know Casey Tessler?"

"Seen Tessler around town a few times. Why, you figure it was Tessler mixed up in that scuffle, marshal?"

"Could have been most anybody. I want you to

94

come down to my office and try to draw a general description of the men who paid this preacher a visit."

"Ain't much of a hand at drawing, marshal, but I'll be there."

With Rain Lonigan as he crossed the lobby went a deeper concern for the missing Casey Tessler. That preacher, Thaddeus Beecher, had been at last night's dance, and sparking Dalphine Wickland. Perhaps the same men who'd paid the preacher a visit at this hotel had appeared at Moseby's Dance Emporium, to have Beecher leave with them. Then to have Casey take off after them. If, as the desk clerk had just told him, these other men were hardcases, their presence would have only served to arouse Casey Tessler's curiosity. Thaddeus Beecher had been in Squaw Gap going on two, three weeks. Perhaps to get to know intimately the time schedule over at the bank. Or to find out just when the Northern Pacific would be carrying gold bullion. These thoughts were fueled by other facts he'd found out about the traveling preacher, such as Beecher's obvious interest in women and the fact he drank hard liquor up in his hotel room. Certainly any man had some vices. But it was becoming clear to Rain Lonigan that for Beecher this could be the man's way of living. What he should have done, and would do once he carried out this errand of getting the visitors from Bismarck a room, was to frame a telegram detailing the general description of Thaddeus Beecher and fire it off to other law enforcement officers.

"Arty Greenway would have done this some time ago. Well, I'm not Greenway . . . just a rancher trying to become a lawman."

A few months after the unexpected death of her husband, Dalphine Wickland had taken in washing along with trying to sell some of her needlework to local merchants. Then she'd hired on as a waitress at the Claremont Hotel. In time she'd overcome her shyness, found that she enjoyed talking to railroad passengers dropping in while their train took on water and coal, and to locals and the ranchers and cowhands. During the spring roundup, which would keep cattlemen out on their ranches, and on into early summer, her hours would be cut, but coming onto fall Dalphine would get in a full week of waitressing. For a while she had considered moving to either Dickinson or Bismarck, where jobs were more plentiful. And where there were more eligible bachelors. Then, and much to her surprise and in church, Thaddeus Beecher had entered her life.

"Ah, ma'am, I asked for some more coffee."

"Oh, excuse me," exclaimed Dalphine Wickland. She brought the spout of the coffee pot over the rim of the cup and refilled it as an embarrassed smile reddened her cheeks. Turning away from the two men seated at the table, she passed among other tables to refill other cups.

Every table was occupied in the dining room at the Claremont Hotel, while those waiting to eat had formed a line out into the lobby. Extra waitresses had been taken on for the Fourth of July weekend festivities. And all of them wore gingham dresses and white aprons. But the thoughts of Dalphine Wickland were elsewhere, with her glance often striking out through the windows facing onto Barcome Street and a hoped for glimpse of Thaddeus Beecher. For he'd come to her home last night, and though Dalphine knew it had been sinful, she'd let him spend the night.

"Married to a preacher," she murmured silently, wonderingly. "Will that ever happen?" A worried afterthought: I hope and pray so.

Every morning with the arrival of the circus the yonkers of Squaw Gap had shown up, to partake of the few rides and other games of amusement, but mostly to gawk at the wild animals in their barred cages. Tiring of this, Marcus Oberlander and two of his age he hung out with would cut westward along Horse Head Creek. Usually they'd swim away the long mornings or once in a while try their luck at fishing. Further adventures had come late yesterday afternoon when the yonkers had stolen through the thick underbrush shielding the creek to suddenly come upon a campfire tended by hardeyed men.

But this morning to their dismay they found only a few dying embers in the small campfire and no hardcases but a lot of empty whiskey bottles and other debris. Grimacing his displeasure, Marcus Oberlander said, "They weren't cowhands."

"Bet they were."

"They were outlaws."

"Yeah," ventured the third yonker, "bet they was at that. Maybe the Pecos Kid?"

"The Pecos Kid," heckled one, "hangs out down in Colorado."

"But they was outlaws."

All three eyed one another in solemn agreement, and then bending down, Marcus Oberlander scooped up an empty whiskey bottle and flung it into the creek. Quickly they found small stones to sling them at the floating bottle until it shattered and sank. Then the organ music coming from the circus drew them back to retrace their trail amongst the trees and underbrush, and with Marcus Oberlander out front.

A crow cawing as it winged away from a low bush almost touching waterline drew Marcus's eyes to it. He yelled, "Scat!"

Only to pull up short when he'd moved closer, and then to stiffen in fear, as another yonker called out, "What's wrong, Marcus?"

"A . . . a body . . ."

The other yonkers crowded in behind Marcus Oberlander, to place hesitant eyes upon the body of Casey Tessler wedged against a fallen cottonwood. The body floated face down, arms outstretched, the lower part of it bobbing under the surface. With eyes still bulging their fear the yonkers bolted as one around another tree and tore upward through underbrush and toward the welcoming buildings of Squaw Gap.

"We've gotta find the marshal!"

"Who was it?"

"Dunno."

"Maybe them outlaws done the killing?"

"Dunno . . . gotta find Marshal Lonigan."

Chapter Ten

A bunch of cowhands heading for Squaw Gap brought their horses into a walk to gaze at a passenger train sweeping into view. Some of them waved as the engineer sounded the train whistle, and one said, "Sure enough a fancy train."

"It ought to be, Mac. That's the North Coast Limited."

Johnston Pettigrew was one of those looking out at the sweeping reach of the Dakota Badlands. Soon they'd reach Squaw Gap, where Pettigrew and the woman he expected to marry would leave the train. But there was in his eyes the unfocused glimmer of a man deep in thought. Mostly this had been brought about by the unexpected appearance of Ella Farnsworth. To his surprise she'd been cordial, had thrown no accusations at him. Her offhand remark about roses had at the time, and now, brought to mind a couple of lines from Robert Burns' A Red Red Rose, "O my Luve's Like a Red Red Rose. That's newly sprung in June . . ."

Reflecting back on it, Johnston Pettigrew was almost sorry he'd run out on Ella. For she was still a beautiful and desirable woman, but unfortunately, married to someone else. Over the years as Pettigrew enhanced his political power there'd been other women. He'd left a trail of broken trysts from one corner of Montana to another, and in doing so had made a lot of enemies. It didn't matter now, now that he was on his way to Washington City. Once they reached the Twin Cities the woman with him, Rose Dumont, would become his wife. In his heart Pettigrew knew he was fond of Rose, but that he did not love her, nor had he ever loved the other women he'd loved and ran out on. But Rose Dumont was monied, would inherit upon the death of her aging father a considerable fortune. And to Johnston Pettigrew money and political power was the name of the game.

"You seem . . . far away, my husband to be."

He reached for her hand and said quietly, "Just wondering if I'm up to this business of representing Montana at our nation's capital."

"You'll do just fine, Johnston," she beamed. "I love you so."

"As I love you."

He felt a lessening in speed before the conductor came into their car to announce the next stop would be Squaw Gap, and somewhat anxiously Pettigrew swung his eyes back to the window and the place he'd be getting off at sliding into his range of vision. Pettigrew knew their baggage would be waiting for them once they detrained, and the money he'd passed to the conductor would ensure that the North Coast Limited would grind to a halt with the observation car opposite the depot platform. And it was through this car that he brought Rose Dumont and out onto the open observation platform at its rear. At Johnston Pettigrew's appearance, the marching band of Squaw Gap struck up a stirring rendition of Pettigrew's campaign song, Zebra Dun, this being one of the old cowboy songs.

Over the boisterous cheers of those with him the mayor of Squaw Gap yelled, "Welcome to Squaw Gap, Senator Pettigrew."

Smiling, and with his arm around Rose Dumont, he responded with, "If the truth be known I'm not a senator—not yet. But on behalf of Miss Dumont . . . whom I shall marry in the near future . . . we want to thank the citizens of this wonderful town for asking us to be here for this patriotic weekend."

"Glad to have you," shouted Mayor Armond Weaver. "Now make way here, folks, for our distinguished guest. Senator Pettigrew, we have a special carriage waiting to take you folks over to the Claremont Hotel. And here, Senator, is what we've got scheduled for you. Yessir, Senator Pettigrew, a fine day for all of us here at Squaw Gap."

Back along the fringes of the crowd lingered the man known in Squaw Gap as Preacher Thaddeus Beecher. A sardonic smile curled up one corner of his mouth, though in his eyes there was a cold and pondering glint. His brothers and the others here to kill Pettigrew were waiting somewhat impatiently at one of the livery stables, their horses saddled, and at the insistence of gunhand Tanner McKitrick, without any whiskey at hand. This was not the time, he'd insisted, to have their firing guns go awry because they were liquored up. Celebrating would come later, and westward in Montana someplace.

"Beecher, seems we keep running into one another."

He slid an eye to the left to take in the editor of the *Squaw Gap Chronicle*. "Appears we do."

"A happy day for this cowtown."

"Folks hereabouts deserve a little happiness. 'Cause this is rugged country to make a living in."

"It is that, sir."

"How come, Mr. Paulson, you're not up there hobnobbing with the illustrious Senator Johnston Pettigrew?"

"As I said before, Mr. Beecher, I've heard it all a thousand times. Oh, I'll put in the *Chronicle* the gist of what the illustrious senator will spout out later, etc, etc. Until then I'll have to endure one of those having dinner with Pettigrew over at the Claremont Hotel."

"I wrangled an invitation too."

"Meaning I'm not the only one liking a free dinner?"

They fell into step, with Tanner McKitrick saying, "Never pass up an invite 'cause a man in my line of work never knows where that next meal is coming from."

Rain Lonigan had managed to steal a few moments from his duties as town marshal to have an early noon meal with his family over at the Claremont Hotel. As they left the dining room and paused under the covered arcade fronting the hotel, Rain handed his son and daughter, Sara, some coins. "Remember, candy is bad for your teeth."

"Daddy, you always tells us that."

"Now, Sara," said Jillian Lonigan, "your father's right. Make sure you keep an eye on your brother over at that circus." She watched her children hurry away. "Well, honey, I suppose you have to go back to work."

"What I'm getting paid to do. But not for too much longer. You going over to Doc Barcome's?"

"Lydia asked me over. Then we'll be back around one o'clock to hear what this politician from Montana has to say."

"I'll be watching for you." Rain waited until his wife had rounded the corner onto a side street before he scanned what was going on along Barcome Street. A couple of blocks upstreet he spotted one of his deputies coming out of a saloon. During the day he wanted them scattered out, so as to cover all of the saloons and other places where drinks were served. But of particular concern to Rain at the moment was a place that had caused him trouble in the past, this being Jake Mulligan's Red Dot Casino. Ever since the casino owner's wife had run off with a drifting gambler, Mulligan had sort of let go. It wasn't so much that Jake Mulligan ran a crooked game as it was that the Red Dot had become a hangout for local toughs, a few girls of the line, and just possibly those who rode outside the law. Just thinking of heading over there had taken Rain's thoughts away from cowpoke Casey Tessler, and he was almost at the end of Barcome Street and cutting up Elm when resounding his way came the Squaw

Gap band parading toward the Claremont Hotel. This, and a few shouted hurrahs, popping of firecrackers, the din of a cowtown packed tight as wet buckskin drying in the sun.

"Rain!"

Breaking stride, he swung around as a deputy, Glen Adock, trotted toward him, and Rain said, "Another runaway horse?"

"Some kids busted into your office telling me they found a body down by the creek."

"You sure?"

"They was scared . . . all jabbering together. But no question about it."

"Let's check it out," responded Rain Lonigan, as surfacing came new worries about Casey Tessler. They threaded through the crowd gathered near the Claremont Hotel, and went beyond to the town jail. The door was open and Rain passed inside to lay his eyes upon Marcus Oberlander standing by his desk. "You sure about this, son?"

"Yessir, marshal. It was just floating there . . . down in the water."

"A man?"

"Yessir . . . floating face down."

Nodding, Rain said quietly, "Marcus, I want you to take us back there. You other boys, keep quiet about this. Go home now. But I'll want to talk to you later." As two of the yonkers scampered out, he questioned Marcus Oberlander to find out the body lay where Horse Head Creek ox-bowed back to the south. Then he told his deputy to find the undertaker.

With Marcus Oberlander taking two strides for

his one, Marshal Lonigan moved out of the alley behind the jail to pass along a narrow lane cutting toward the creek. Left of them were the gaudy tents and booths of the circus and people trekking toward it or back to the main street. Once they cleared the Borden house, a ramshackle building where old man Borden sat kind of huddled on the front porch steps as though his aging thoughts had drawn him elsewhere, and his untidy woodpile with moss sticking to the pieces of wood and an axe showing rust, at Marcus's insistence they cut under an elm tree to work their way through thickets passing down the loamy creek bank.

"Right about here, marshal."

"Son, you wait right here . . . under that tree. If you spot my deputy, wave him on in."

Rain went on, pushing thorny branches aside, and with the few pussy willow stems he brushed against casting their white seeds at his worn Levis. He ignored the mud clinging to his boots as the fallen cottonwood as described by the yonkers appeared, and then Rain saw the floating body, to be gripped with a deep feeling of grief and disbelief.

"Casey . . . no . . ."

He waded out into brackish waters almost touching the barrel of his holstered sidearm and pulled the body closer. With a bitter reluctance he turned the body over and floated it closer to the bank, as all the while his pain-wracked eyes took in a face he'd come to love and respect. Somehow Rain managed to lift the body onto a grassy stretch of ground, and where he went to his knees to gather Casey Tessler in his arms. He'd spotted the back wound, and from what the hotel clerk over at the Starbuck Hotel had told him, knew that Casey had been murdered there.

"But . . . why? Casey . . . why?"

Chapter Eleven

The youngest McKitrick brother clamped his hands on a barrel out behind the livery stable and leaned over it as his eyes went glassy. Sucking in his stomach, he made a retching sound like a coyote being struck broadside by a 30.06 slug. Spraying out of his gaping mouth came a yellowish, blue-tinted gore. A bellyache caused by steady bouts with the bottle ever since hitting Squaw Gap and bad food had kept Blaine McKitrick up most of the night. Mercifully, Tanner McKitrick had hiked over to a mercantile store opening just after sunrise. He came back with a concoction of rum and creosote into which he had added a couple of raw eggs, forced the suffering Blaine McKitrick to chug-a-lug this remedy damned near at gunpoint. Eyes lidding over, his face going yellow as a Chinaman's, Blaine had managed to lurch outside, where he'd spent most of the morning, either cursing his brother Tanner or heaving himself over the barrel and cleansing out his innards.

What troubled Tanner, and Wade McKitrick, was that at best their brother had a surly frame of mind, and was somewhat unreliable. Blaine would be in a killing mood, which suited Tanner's fancy. His concern was that Blaine would unlimber that Colts and start blazing away before they'd ridden into place along Barcome Street. Then, and knowing Johnston Pettigrew, the politician would abandon that speaker's platform and his current belle and not even leave heel markings as he sought safer territory. He voiced his concern to Wade taking his dreamy ease on a rickety chair up by the closed front doors.

"You'd think he'd learn by now."

"Trouble was pa up and died when we was all too young . . . and if you remember, Tanner, you wasn't around to wetnurse the rest of us."

"I would have probably dumped all of you in a gunny sack and headed for Rainy Creek."

"At times pa had the same notion." He lifted a leg to place it elegantly over another, let a hand drape down to spin the big silver-gleaming Mex rowel on his size nine Juston. At the moment Wade McKitrick didn't have a worry in the world, though there was some concern for Blaine camped out back. A corner of his mouth curling impishly, Wade cut loose with a loud fart, lifted one hind cheek Tanner's way. "A steady diet of prairie strawberries will do that to a man."

"With you it comes natural." Tanner McKitrick, slouched against a stable partition, allowed the sober set to his longish face to break into amused crinkles. There was a brief temptation to pass rancid air as Wade had just done, but quickly the moment of humor was driven away by thoughts of what the next hour would bring. Deliberately he turned his eyes to dependable Brent Wilmar checking out the action on his Smith & Wesson; not a great hand with a gun but always there backing the play of the McKitricks. Next came Larry Madden hunkered down in the same stall with Wilmar, and with the Texan rolling another smoke. A cool one, and the bogus preacher felt more at ease. His eyes flicked on to Smithly and Jesse Cairne hunkered down by a pile of straw, Cairne dealing from a greasy deck, and the other hardcase sweeping in the cards to have his long fingers close avariciously around them. Neither trusted the other. He knew that Smithly had been blooded, one killing down in the Nations, probably others elsewhere. Today it would be Cairne's turn to get his cherry busted.

"Why did you take on Cairne?"

"He was available."

"Petty thiefs and muggers are a dime a dozen."

Wade McKitrick reached back and rubbed the nape of his neck, then he stretched lazily and said, "Maybe folks hereabouts will be satisfied if we leave a couple of bodies behind."

"For damned sure you're my brother," Tanner said quietly. "A double eagle Cairne soils his pants after he breaks his cherry."

"Give me three to one on that and you've got a bet. Now unlimber that big turnip."

Tanner McKitrick lifted from his fob pocket his watch. "A little after one." He stepped up to a front window and peered out at Barcome Street stretching eastward. He could see a crowd gathered before the Clairborne Hotel and others hovering on the boardwalks, and a bunch up on the speaker's platform. Without turning he said, "Appears the mayor's still jawing away. We'll head out at one-thirty."

"Suits me." Wade McKitrick smiled as he tipped his Stetson low over his forehead and snuggled

110

deeper on the rickety chair.

Marshal Rain Lonigan and his deputy trailed after the undertaker bringing his wagon away from the creek. They'd rolled up the body in an old blanket, and it was Rain's intentions to go over to the funeral parlor and make sorrowful arrangements for Casey Tessler's burial. Afterward he figured on having a word with that preacher, Thaddeus Beecher.

"By now," Rain said, "there should have been a response to that wire I sent out on Beecher."

"If Beecher isn't guilty of anything other places, I doubt if anybody will bother to wire back."

"You're probably right," said Rain Lonigan, as behind him the yonker who'd brought him here emerged from the underbrush.

Still lodged in Marcus Oberlander's thoughts was the fear of what had just happened, and that he hadn't told the marshal about those gunhands being camped along the creek. "They're the murderers," he blurted out, while glancing around half-expecting to be accosted by one of the killers. "Can't tell my pa about this; marshal's orders." Suddenly, his face brightening, he broke into a shambling run. "The preacher . . . Reverend Beecher . . . he'll know what to do."

Framing a scowl, one Diamond T cowhand glanced at another and drawled, "This longwinded bullcrap ain't for me. If it hadn't of been for that pretty thing up there shifting her legs from time to

111

time I'd have hauled ass out of here."

"That Pettigrew's woman is a sassy looker all right. But I was sighting a little higher on that red dress she's a-wearing."

"Yup," agreed the other, "them's some nice knockers."

The loud phlegmy baritone of country commissioner Ezzard Gilmoure silenced the pair of cowhands and seemed to stir an overhanging banner as he continued on with his address taken from various parts of the Constitution. Once while expelling air a button had popped on the bright red and white vest stretched over his ample belly, then shortly thereafter another. But gripped by a patriotic fever, this helped along by the five snifters of brandy he'd had at that free dinner over at the Claremont Hotel, he'd rambled on to include without realizing it a few sage chestnuts from the works of Mark Twain. This had brought some snickering laughter and a few catcalls, which had only served to make local politician and half-hearted rancher Ezzard Gilmoure rattle on louder. He was sucking air into his tiring lungs when a hand clamped upon his broad shoulder.

Whispered Mayor Armond Weaver, "That last line, dammit, was from Pilgrim's Progress. You've got a minute to wind this up."

"And in closing, my dear friends," went on Gilmoure just as gustily, "I bring you back again to the heroic deeds of our forefathers as they fought for liberty."

"I hope old Gilmoure don't go back any further."

"He just might . . ."

"In concluding, therefore, I say our forefathers have given us a grand heritage . . . the blessings of the Almighty . . . and just remember, my dear friends, that I will be opposing our fair mayor in this fall's elections. A vote for Gilmoure is a vote for progress." Dabbing with a checkered handkerchief at his perspiring forehead, county commissioner Gilmoure stumbled around under the glaring eyes of the present mayor and managed to reclaim his chair to scattered applause and more catcalls, and to the backs of some leaving.

The incumbent mayor, sparks flinting out of his red-veined eyes, black double-breasted frock coat flaring open as he hustled forward, planted his hands palm down on the speaker's stand and uttered somewhat disdainfully, "The last speaker, the illustrious Ezzard Gilmoure, is, as you know, about to put his hardscrabble spread on the auction block." He revealed a smug porcelain smile, then his false teeth clacked together. "Now ladies and gents, it's only fitting and proper I present to you one of the founders of your fair city . . . and without further ado here is Doc D.B. Barcome."

Rising to shuffle forward as the mayor sat down, Doc Barcome said quickly, "As you know pushing pills and such is what I do best. But for some insufferable reason the Fourth of July committee insisted I have the honor of introducing the illustrious senator from Montana, that being Johnston Pettigrew."

About a half hour ago Doc Barcome had ambled over from his office, where he'd seen a few patients, and the only effort he'd made to tidy up was to put on an old tie. The gray suit hung

113

limply on his middle-aged frame, and now from under the brim of a felt hat he looked about at many he knew. His eyes went past the editor of the *Squaw Gap Chronicle* to the wife of Marshal Lonigan, Jillian, to the fringes of the crowd and that traveling preacher, Thaddeus Beecher, emerging from a distant livery stable with a saddle horse. Beyond Beecher he spotted a pair of riders emerging from behind the stable and crossing the street and then disappear. Striking a wondering finger along his graying temple, Doc Barcome said, "Well, you all know me, that I'm kind of short when it comes to making a jackass out of myself at shindigs of this kind. Folks, with great pleasure I present the honorable Johnston Pettigrew." He swung away from the speaker's stand and began applauding with the others.

Before rising, Johnston Pettigrew said quietly to the woman at his side, "My first duty will be to tell this gathering of our intentions to marry."

"Please, Johnston," she blushed, "you don't have to do that."

A reassuring hand touched her knee, then Pettigrew swept up from the chair and strode the short distance to plant himself before the speaker's stand. The applause regained momentum when he raised his arms over his head and flashed that toothy smile. And then he swept the new Stetson from his head to have afternoon sunlight dust his blondish hair. He set the hat on the stand and broke out with, "It is indeed an honor to be here to help all of you celebrate such a glorious day."

The sonorous tones of Johnston Pettigrew soon quieted a few hecklers, brought the crowd surging in closer, as he spoke of the common problems shared by territorial Montana and the Dakotas.

"So, after being duly elected by my peers, I'm off to Washington City. Permit me at this point to introduce"—he swung around—"my betrothed, and a woman who has won my heart, the beautiful Rose Dumont." He extended his hand to have her rise and step forward.

Chapter Twelve

Tanner McKitrick led his gray bronc upstreet toward the Claremont Hotel and the man he was about to kill. Snugged under his somber black coat was a Navy Colts, the tip of the worn leather holster barely showing. Where he was, about two blocks from the hotel, had little pedestrian traffic, though the saloons he passed still held a lot of diehard drinkers or gamblers. He'd gotten rid of the Bible, but strapped to the inside of his left forearm in a special holster was an English pepper box revolver, a bronzed weapon just under eight inches in length.

McKitrick's face was unruffled, and he walked easily as of someone looking for a place to tie up his horse. He passed through an empty intersection, and then in the next block, hung back a little until he spotted Jesse Cairne and Larry Madden and his brother, Blaine, riding his way in a wide gap between two buildings facing onto Barcome Street. Now Tanner McKitrick swung aboard the bronc, slowly, let himself get the feel of the saddle before having the bronc step out at a walk. From his saddle he could see Wade, Smithly, and Brent Wilmar, just reining onto the street farther to the east, and separating, Wade coming down the middle, the others close to the boardwalks.

It had been agreed after some heated debate with Wade that he would have the more dangerous job of pressing into the crowd and coming in at the speaker's platform from the front. It would be easier to go for Pettigrew from there, and afterward his woman. He knew that Wade would rely on his Henry as he shared in the killing of Pettigrew, and with Blaine, the hardcases, hammering away at the crowd.

With a pleasant smile plucking at his lips, Tanner McKitrick began edging his horse through the press of those listening to the politician from Montana. There were a few smiles in return, some wondering glances for the horseman. He managed to bring his horse to the western wall of the Claremont Hotel, beyond which the people were packed in too tight, and he murmured, "This will have to do."

But he still made no effort to draw his Colts as he slouched in the saddle and tipped a cautionary finger to Wade McKitrick just reining up and laying a hand on the butt of his sheathed rifle. The agreed upon signal was for the others to wait until Tanner McKitrick had removed his black hat and then settled it back on his head. What he wanted now was for the man who'd doublecrossed them back in Montana to lock glances, to know the McKitricks had caught up with him. So for the moment he let Johnston Pettigrew ramble on. He let his eyes drift to the woman seated on the platform, and back to fix on the face of Pettigrew.

"So again I tell you that we must protect our

freedoms . . . that we . . ." Johnston Pettigrew's voice faltered as his eyes spanned across the street at Tanner McKitrick. A wild gleam came into his eyes, one mingled with fear and disbelief. A glance upstreet revealed three more horsemen, and others in the crowd also spotted Wade McKitrick and those with him.

"Vengeance is ours!" cried out Tanner McKitrick as he doffed his hat, and as he reached for his holstered revolver he felt someone pawing at his left arm.

"Reverend Beecher . . . I have to talk to you," exclaimed Marcus Oberlander. "I was looking all over for you . . . please, you gotta hear me out . . ."

Wade McKitrick's rifle boomed to stagger Pettigrew. Other weapons sounded as Tanner McKitrick pulled out his Navy Colts, and with a scowl twisting up his face, he brought the weapon passing above the saddle horn and placed a leaden slug in the forehead of the boy, Marcus, to have him crumble away. His horse plunging, he brought the Colts to bear upon Johnston Pettigrew trying to come down off the platform, and with the man's left coat sleeve streaked with blood. He put two slugs into Pettigrew's chest, grimaced when the man toppled off the platform, cut loose with another slug at the woman just rising in shocked disbelief to have Rose Dumont spin sideways.

There was still enough time for Johnston Pettigrew, sprawled dying in front of the speaker's platform, to focus his eyes on a woman wearing a reddish dress scattering as others were doing, and he said incoherently, "Why . . . Ella . . . I know

118

you . . . you're behind this? A rose . . . that's it . . . forgot to give you a . . . rose." A moment later he died.

Westward on the fringes of the crowd Blaine McKitrick had scored a few hits, two men and an older gent trying to hobble away with the use of a cane. His horse rearing and spinning around, Blaine McKitrick managed to bring it under control as he sighted in on two women just reaching the boardwalk and the front door of a mercantile store. He snapped off a careless shot, grinned when one of the women suddenly clutched at her back and went down. He pulled the trigger again only to have the hammer slam onto an empty chamber, and then Tanner McKitrick was cantering past him and yelling, "Come on you damned fools! Let's not overstay our welcome."

All four of them passed down that wide gap between the buildings and found the alley running to the west. Glancing back, Tanner McKitrick saw that Smithly was slumped over and holding onto his saddle horn. In one smooth movement he brought up his Navy Colts and placed a slug in the center of Smithly's weathered hat. Though the hardcase dropped out of the saddle his bronc kept after the others clearing some more buildings before pounding over the railroad tracks and riding at a gallop for a ravine quartering away to the northwest. The ravine, they knew from having scouted it out, would bring them deeper into the Badlands and back to the railroad right-of-way, where they'd cut the telegraph wire. Halfway through the ravine, a wave of the arm from Tanner McKitrick brought them reining up. A short while later the others pounded in, Wade McKitrick laughing as he threw everyone a crazy-eyed look.

"It went just like you said, Tanner," he chortled. "You should have seen the look on Pettigrew's face."

"You think they'll get up a posse?"

"Right now they still don't know what hit them, Will. But after we cut that telegraph wire, we'll keep to the saddle. Cut down south to come out by that Powder River country. Look up an old acquaintance at Broadus."

"You mean Dirty Jake Turley?"

"Yup, Wade. We'll resupply at his place. Maybe hole up for a couple of days to rest the horses."

"Then on to Bozeman and the rest of the money," smiled Blaine McKitrick.

"Just maybe," said Wade, "I'll run into Frank Modahl. I owe the bastard for what he done to me down in Wyoming."

Impatiently Tanner McKitrick spurred his gray into a canter. Wade McKitrick came up alongside as the others stretched out behind, and he said, "If we do run into Modahl, maybe he can tell us who's been bankrolling this operation. Got me this hunch it hasn't been Lydel Farnsworth."

"His wife, maybe?"

"Yeah, she has reasons to want Pettigrew gunned down. As I recall she spent more time in Pettigrew's bed than he did. And that money better be waiting for us."

"Only a damned fool would hold out on the McKitricks. Wade, I figure it best we ease into Bozeman quietlike; leave the same way. But enough of Bozeman. We've got hard riding ahead of us. After what happened they'll be after us, along with every lawman in Montana once word gets out about Pettigrew. But I'd do it again just to see that look on his face."

Chapter Thirteen

When that rifle had sounded and Johnston Pettigrew had clutched at his arm, the mayor of Squaw Gap and Doc Barcome found themselves trying to protect Rose Dumont. But too late when she tried to help Pettigrew only to be struck in the midriff. Then other guns began rattling, and women and children screamed as panic spread along Barcome Street.

"It was that preacher?" yelled Mayor Weaver.

"And some friends of his." An errant bullet struck the platform near Doc Barcome's hand, and he swung his eyes to the east. "By God, they're shooting into the crowd."

"Johnston . . . please I must help . . ."

"Easy, woman," said Doc Barcome as he saw that the bullet had lodged more in her side, and he looked up at Weaver. "Once they clear out we'll carry her over to my office."

"Why, Doc . . . why are they doing this?"

"I don't know, Armond. Maybe it's Pettigrew they were after."

Down on the patch of ground fronting onto the platform, editor Earl Paulson managed to crawl over and grip the hand of the politician from Montana, to have Pettigrew blurt out something, then go limp. About a dozen others had dropped down by the platform once the shooting commenced. Just past the Claremont Hotel a cowhand caught a slug in his thigh. He fell heavily, but another waddy was there with a helping hand. One of Squaw Gap's deputy marshals drew down on one of the horsemen with his Smith & Wesson bucking in his hand. The deputy missed, but Wade McKitrick didn't, and the deputy clutched at his arm while pushing back against a wall.

The reverberating pounding of gunfire reached Marshal Rain Lonigan about to take his leave from Jenkin's Funeral Parlor, and with Glen Adock exclaiming, "That's too loud to be firecrackers, Rain." He headed outside followed by Rain Lonigan, where they broke running down the narrow side street. A woman screamed, and they could hear shouting amongst the scattering bursts of gunfire.

"Jillian . . . she's out there . . ."

They were almost to Barcome Street when four horsemen swept westerly through the joining of the streets, but long enough for Rain to recognize one of them as Reverend Thaddeus Beecher. Then he came out onto Squaw Gap's main street, only to hold back as did Adock when they realized a few locals and cowpunchers were firing at the riders just swinging in behind a building. And only then did the firing stop. Though a lot of people had made it into or behind buildings lining the street, those unfortunate to come under the attack of the ambushers were picking themselves up. Much to Rain's puzzled dismay he could see four bodies still sprawled in the street, four men and a woman. Up by the speaker's platform Rain could make out Earl Paulson placing his suit coat over the face of a man who'd been killed, and the mayor and Doc Barcome helping Rose Dumont down off the platform.

"Rain, hold up," called out Arty Greenway. Greenway had his marshal's badge pinned to his gray woolen shirt. "All hell suddenly broke loose. I expected you to be here."

Flintily Rain Lonigan replied, "I found Casey Tessler's body out by the creek."

"Casey?"

"It must have happened last night, Arty. Have you seen my wife?"

"In all this confusion, Rain, I can't be sure."

"She was over visiting Doc Barcome's wife. But they planned to come down and watch the festivities."

Glen Adock reached over and gripped Rain's shoulder, and Adock said quietly, "Here comes Dalphine Wickland; never seen that woman with tears in her eyes before."

One glance at the woman coming uncertainly toward him and a chill swept through Rain Lonigan. He took a few tentative steps in her direction, not wanting to ask about his wife, but filled with the certain knowledge that something had happened to Jillian. Dalphine Wickland didn't utter a word as she came up to Rain Lonigan and slipped an arm around his neck, but he could feel the tears falling onto his cheek.

"Marshal . . . Rain . . . your wife is . . ."

"No!" That word seemed to tear out of his heart.

"Jillian was shot in the back. They have her

over by Thompson's store. She's . . ."

He pulled away and went blindly downstreet. He didn't hear people calling out to him or the moans of those who'd been hit by gunfire and were clinging to life. He fought to keep control of himself, and then Doc Barcome's wife, Lydia, saw him coming and rose from where she'd been tending to Rain's wife, with those standing nearby drawing back. Nearly twenty years as a doctor's wife had hardened Lydia Barcome to such mundane things as broken bones and gunshot wounds, and operations. But there was grief staining her ashy face, and with her graying hair mussed up this way she looked a lot older. Drying blood stained the long sleeves of her blue dress.

Lydia Barcome said plainly, "When the shooting started, Rain, we tried for Thompson's. Were just about inside when Jillian got hit in the back. Rain, she's barely alive."

"Where's Doc?" he lashed out.

"Tending to others who've been wounded. But there's a doctor from Dickinson come here for the weekend. Some men are taking off the back door of the store. Then we'll have Jillian carried over to Doc's office."

He brushed past Lydia Barcome and knelt down by his wife. She lay so still that at first Rain thought she'd breathed her last, but the slight rise and fall of her ribcage told him otherwise. Reaching for her hand, Rain Lonigan brought his lips down and kissed her fingers, and he said, "I didn't need this job all that bad, honey. Seems Casey was right . . . about that traveling preacher. Please . . . please don't die on me . . ."

A hand touched his shoulder. "Rain, we have to move her."

With a bitter reluctance he left go of Jillian's hand and came erect. He stepped out of the way while trying to choke down this growing sense of rage as folks he knew placed his wife's inert form on the wooden door. Then he followed behind when the four men trudged upstreet. Falling in beside Rain was Lydia Barcome, who said, "Doc'll do the best he can, Rain."

"I . . . know that, Mrs. Barcome. She got hit in the back?"

"Along her backbone, unfortunately. Low enough so that it might have done harm to the baby she's carrying."

"Marshal," yelled one of Rain's deputies, "we need you over here."

"Go ahead, Rain," said Lydia Barcome, "tend to your duties. Don't worry, if Jillian's condition worsens, we'll send for you." When he hesitated, she added, "there's nothing you can do over there anyway."

"Guess you're right," he said numbly, to have Rain Lonigan swerve out into the street toward Glen Adock and others including the editor of the *Squaw Gap Chronicle.* Shouldering in, Rain found they were clustered around one of those who'd been killed. Rain inquired sharply, "How many got gunned down?"

Adock said, "Four killed outright including that Montana politician."

"Five more packing bullet wounds," said Earl Paulson.

"Damn," Rain muttered as he bent over and

lifted a corner of the sheet covering the body. "Luther Neilsen . . . never had an unkind word for anybody."

"Marshal, we're sorry about Casey Tessler too. But had to be the same ones who did this."

"It must have been that Casey finally remembered where he'd seen that preacher before. Which he damn-well isn't."

"We're gonna have to get up a posse and go after them."

"Count me out."

"But you're the marshal?"

"Arty Greenway's your duly appointed marshal," said Rain as his eyes hardened. "Right now I don't know if my wife is gonna live or die . . . as she was one of those who got gunned down."

"Rain . . . we're sorry," said Earl Paulson. "I guess all we can do right now is bury those who got killed. Think about exacting justice later. Go to your wife, Rain."

He gazed out past the soft glow of lamplight to fireflies dancing through elm trees as around Rain Lonigan the town of Squaw Gap was strangely muted. The screened back porch contained a small round table and several cane chairs. The sky had clouded some, hiding the moon but there was starlight. About a half-hour ago he'd been told by the editor of the *Squaw Gap Chronicle* that it was a quarter after ten, but to Rain it seemed a lot later. Others had come and gone, passing back through Doc Barcome's one-story clinic or using the back door.

"I'm glad," he said to Earl Paulson, "that Pettigrew's woman is going to make it."

"So are the others who were hit by gunfire."

"The savagery of it all," remarked Mayor Armond Weaver, who couldn't keep to a chair but kept pacing around, an unlit cigar clamped between his teeth, and a stubble of beard darkening his round face. "The way that preacher gunned down the Oberlander boy. The question is, could we have done something to prevent this. I'm not blaming you, Rain."

"Nor should you blame anyone else, Armond," said Paulson. "They came here to kill Johnston Pettigrew . . . for what reason I don't know." As he picked up his coffee cup, the sight of Dalphine Wickland coming up the back walkway brought him up to go over and open the screen door, to let in a few determined flies.

"Thank you," she said. Moving up to the table, she placed on it a platter covered by a lacy cloth. "How . . . how is it going with Jillian?"

"She's still alive," responded Rain.

Dalphine folded onto a chair and brought a hand up to brush a tear away from an eye. "I'm so sorry. You see, Rain, I let that man, Beecher, come into my house. I . . . I feel so unclean." In her eyes there was a silent plea, and more tears.

"To you he was a preacher, Dalphine. I suppose he's done this before, in lots of other places." Rain placed an empty cup before her, filled it with coffee from the big blue enamel pot. "I'm just hoping we'll receive a response to those wires I sent out on Beecher."

The shock of what had happened to Jillian had

passed, to be replaced by a deep bitterness, and this anxiety as Rain waited for word on his wife. Earlier this evening Doc Barcome assisted by another doctor, had operated to remove the bullet from where it was lodged next to Jillian Lonigan's spinal column. Her condition, though, was grave. And it had been explained to Rain that if her condition worsened they would have to perform a caesarean operation in an attempt to save the baby, a medical procedure of cutting through the walls of the abdomen and uterus, and somewhat reluctantly he'd given his consent. Otherwise, Doc Barcome had told Rain, they'd lose the baby. Until this moment, until this shocking thing had happened, Rain hadn't realized just how much Jillian meant to him. The Rocking L would be a lonely place without her. But she had to live, and inwardly a silent prayer gave Rain Lonigan a ray of hope.

Those keeping this long vigil on the back porch looked at one another at the squalling of a newborn baby. A smile came from Earl Paulson as he said to Rain, "Got a lusty pair of lungs."

Despite his fears for Jillian, Rain allowed a smile to flit into his eyes. "Sounds like a boy." He rose and looked through the open inner door opening onto a narrow hallway centering the wide wooden-framed building. His hat lay on the floor by the table, and by force of habit Rain ran a hand through his unruly hair. Then a nurse appeared carrying the baby born to the Lonigans, and with Doc Barcome also coming out of the delivery room.

Only a reddish face showed in the blanketed form carried by the nurse, and she said, "It's a boy, Mr. Lonigan; weighs in at eight pounds."

"My wife?" He lifted his eyes from his new son to Doc Barcome, who also moved out onto the back porch to draw Rain off into a dark corner.

"I'd best come right out with it, Rain," he said wearily, the pain of what he was about to say etched on his face. "She's failing . . ."

"No, Doc, please, there's two of you . . . there's something you can do."

"Rain, please understand," he said gently. "The strain of the pregnancy and Jillian's being shot were more than her body can handle. She lost a lot of blood . . . and she's hemorrhaging . . . probably from a ruptured blood vessel. Right now we've got the bleeding stopped. But more than that, it's her heart, Rain. Jillian's a small woman. How I wish I could tell you otherwise."

"May I see her?"

"You have every right. But she fell into a coma. Come, Rain, I'll take you to your wife."

Two days later and under a light rainfall Rain Lonigan stood holding a handful of earth he'd picked up as he and other mourners watched the casket holding his wife being lowered into the ground. The new graves of others killed on that bloody day were clustered lower on the gentle hillock. The minister of St. Thomas Evangelical Church dropped some dirt on the casket, as did Rain as he tried to contain his grief.

"From dust to dust . . ."

Just behind Rain a woman started crying, and opposite the gravesite the wife of Doc Barcome placed a comforting arm around Dalphine Wickland's quivering shoulders. Rain stood with his left arm clutched around his daughter, with Kiley Lonigan's tears mixed with the falling drops of warm rainwater.

"The Lord giveth . . . and the Lord taketh away . . ."

Rain no longer wore that marshal's badge, as he was clothed in his only suit, black and threadbare at the elbows. After Jillian had passed away, sometime after sunup yesterday morning, he'd let Doc Barcome take charge of things from there, knowing that in his grief he had to ride out alone to collect his embittered thoughts. Somehow he'd found himself riding out to the Rocking L to check on things, there to get his suit and some clothes for his children. He supposed that marshal's badge was still down by the barn, this after he'd torn it from his shirt and tossed it away.

At the moment he had difficulty focusing on any clear thought as the service ended. A buggy awaited them, which he got into with some reluctance, for they were expected to head over to the church for a lunch put on by the ladies of Squaw Gap.

"Daddy, we won't see mom again . . ."

"Only in our memories, son. Here now, it's all right to shed some tears for your mother." As the buggy led out down the slope, Rain looked over at another carriage in which Ben Oberlander and his wife and surviving son were riding. "Guess I'm not the only one who's suffering."

And also yesterday morning Marshal Arty Greenway had headed out with a dozen or so others in an attempt to track down the killers. Rain was of the firm opinion that these men had made good their getaway; the rainfall of today assuring that. Let the rightful marshal of Squaw Gap worry about those killers, because at the moment for Rain Lonigan there would be a time of mourning. Later he would have to find someone to take care of his children, the new addition to the family, the hiring of one or two men to replace Casey Tessler.

Later would come Rain Lonigan's heading out on the vengeance trail, for he was determined to find these killers. A telegram arriving this morning had revealed that three of them were the McKitrick brothers.

"Tanner McKitrick — bogus preacher. You're mine, Tanner, you and your murdering brothers."

Chapter Fourteen

A cloud shadow passed over Rain Lonigan bringing his horse away from the telegraph line strung along the Northern Pacific right-of-way. Just to the east, Squaw Gap was basking under a surly afternoon sun. A week ago they'd buried his wife, and afterward Rain had sought seclusion out at his ranch. Word brought to the Rocking L by a pair of cowhands he'd taken on told of how the McKitricks had gotten away from a posse led by Marshal Arty Greenway.

That night Rain Lonigan had made up his mind to go after the killers. And there was only one man who could help him, a loner with the strange moniker of Canada Reese. The following day Rain had brought Kiley and Sara into Squaw Gap, where his new son was being cared for by Lydia Barcome. After telling her of his intentions, Lydia had said plainly, "You're not a gunhand, Rain. Perhaps you'd better consider your children, that you might be killed."

"Perhaps that would be better than living without my wife."

"Yes," she finally said, "if someone gunned down my husband I'd probably do the same thing. But there is one thing, Rain. I'm going to ask Dalphine Wickland to help care for Kiley and

Sara."

"She's a lonely woman, I reckon."

"More than that, Rain. Word has gotten around about that killing preacher spending some time at her house. Now a lot of Squaw Gap women are calling her a slut and worse."

He'd left then, to make the long trek out to the homestead of Canada Reese and the man's traplines strung along creeks flowing into the Little Missouri River. When the snow began melting and in autumn were the only times the elusive trapper came into Squaw Gap. Before settling into the Badlands of the Dakotas, Canada Reese, so the bar talk went, had been one of those mysterious plainsmen, whose demise was caused by the High Plains Indians being forced onto reservations and the disappearance of the buffalo.

Once while out looking for strays far north of his spread, Rain had stumbled onto Canada Reese hovering over a lonely campfire. He'd been hesitant about riding in, since the man had a reputation for not welcoming visitors out to his place and when sighted always had a big Sharps draped across his saddlehorn. But frost was touching upon the Badlands, and being without provisions of his own, Rain had called out his name and that he was coming in. So he'd done so half-expecting to be cut in two by that Sharps.

When Rain came around a rocky outcropping of a narrow opening in ledges guarding a small glade filled with prairie grass and scrub oak, all he found was a tethered horse and flames lapping at a battered old coffee pot. The long recess was so narrow he could reach out with both arms extended and touch either wall, though ahead the passageway widened to show rain water cascading down into a shimmering pool. But where was Canada Reese?

Gingerly he eased out of the saddle, stood there without making any attempt to close on the campfire. Beyond the pool loomed the back wall of the high ledge, and if he was boxed in, so was the plainsman.

"You're Lonigan."

The voice of the plainsman had come from behind, causing the short hairs at the nape of Rain's neck to stir nervously. Slowly he swung sideways to see Canada Reese crouching out of a small crumbling hole at the base of the east wall, and when the man straightened up, he was about a half-inch shorter than Rain Lonigan at an even six feet. The eyes of Reese were pondering black coals in a gaunt face cut with deep lines trailing under a full beard. A black and white furred ermine cap was pressed down over Reese's graying hair. Hemming down the sleeves of the buckskin coat were faded red and blue stripes, such as squaws would do for their men, and the buckskin trousers touched upon worn boots. He had both a holstered gun and a hunting knife at his waist.

"I was out chasing strays."

"Thought you was a rustler or highwayman," responded Canada Reese, though he'd recognized the rancher but still kept the barrel pointed at the intruder. Shortly thereafter one black-lignite eye lidded down in a sign of welcome as he brushed past Rain, and by the campfire, lowered the Sharps onto his saddle. Hunkering down came natural to the plainsman as he watched Rain tend to unsaddling his bronc, then bring his saddle and bedroll over to lay them down.

"You got a tin cup in that saddlebag?"

"I appreciate your hospitality, Mr. Reese," said Rain as he reached around and opened a saddlebag.

"Canada's the name. I was just fixing to fry me some fresh venison . . . and there'll be beans."

That was how it began, Rain Lonigan bedrolling for the night, and once in a while encountering Canada Reese out in these sunken hills coined the Badlands by the Indian. As well as not being all that fast at drawing a gun, though Rain was a better'n average shot, tracking down those killers would take a sharper eye than his. He could have gone over and hired on Ike Harker, a sometime rancher and oldtime game hunter, but the trouble was Harker had taken to hitting the bottle. So it had to be Canada Reese, who'd heard Rain out and hired on not for the going rate but just for the grub and a chance to see the Great Plains again.

When the telegraph line dropped over a hillock, Rain Lonigan came upon his guide, Reese, up ahead about a half mile, slouched in the saddle and gazing southwesterly. He came up to Reese, who said quietly, "As I said before, Rain, forget them heading east. Or north, I figure. Too bad that rain washed out their trail."

"What do you have in mind, Canada, them heading south, to the Black Hills maybe?"

"Not hardly . . . since they came here to kill that Montana politician."

136

"Then back to Montana," debated Rain.

"But not beelining it. They'll make a big detour, north maybe; but more rugged country thataway."

With his Stetson tipped back, Rain watched as his guide used that sharp hunting knife to slice away some chewing tobacco from a big brown-cured hunk of it. He couldn't help noticing how big Canada's hands were, scarred in places, and dirt showing under the nails of the long thick fingers. It was a high sky they'd be riding under, and into a quartering wind stirring up some dust.

"The trouble is, Canada, we know nothing about the McKitricks."

"Don't have to know much. What they won't be doing"—he got his horse to loping—"is stick to the main roads, at least until they're well into Montana, or even Wyoming. Yonder's Sentinel Butte; another dozen miles we'll be out of the Badlands. Someplace in between we could get lucky and strike their trail or find where they camped."

"Out west farther, they'll have to stop at a town for supplies. A lot of people will remember six outlaws paying them a visit."

They came upon an old trail made by a half dozen or so riders around sundown, one that wended, as Canada had figured, to the southwest. In these parts passing rain showers missed more tracts of land than they touched, and the two men took the time to read each hoofprint in an attempt to pick up any odd horseshoe markings. "Getting too dark to read them," Canada said. "Best we pitch camp; get an early start."

"They seem pretty sure of themselves by not

troubling to hide their trail. Maybe these outlaws didn't pass through here at all, Canada."

"Could be, since I ain't no prophet. But so far this trail is all we've got."

"I've been thinking, about when we hit some cowtown in Montana. It would be a good idea to find out some more about Johnston Pettigrew, like where he hangs his hat, and other things about the man that could help us. Dammit, Canada, I want those killers."

"Expect you do," said Canada Reese as he kneed his roan gelding off to thickets sheltering a natural spring flowing out of a ravine wall. Parting the thickets, he dismounted by a small pool of clear water. He didn't say another word until the horses had been taken care of and he was kneeling by the pool of water and filling the coffee pot. "Had me a squaw once, but back so long ago I plumb forgot what she looked like. Sure liked to crawl under a buffer robe with me . . . or others if I weren't around. One day some Crow raided that Shoshone camp up near Eagle Creek. Anyways, when I got back from a hunting trip she was gone. I expect since I seen her last, Mr. Lonigan, she's slept with half the Crow nation. That sort of put the damper on things as far as squaws was concerned."

Rain knew that the plainsman didn't have the reputation of being a talking man. Or it could be that Canada Reese had to get to know someone before opening up. During the course of a nighting meal of more venison and beans, and biscuits that set a man's teeth to grinding, he'd throw in an occasional word as Reese told of his earlier years, not boasting but in a casual way. It came to Rain after a while that this was Canada Reese's way of helping him take his mind off their reasons for being out here.

"You know, Canada, all I'm hoping is that you can track them down. After that I don't expect you to risk your neck."

"Six gunhands going up against a lonely rancher ain't my idea of seeing your graying years, Rain. Was me, I'd look to some Montana lawmen for help."

This caused Rain Lonigan to remember the marshal's badge he'd packed along. Just before leaving his place, Rain had gone down where he'd thrown the badge away and looked until he found it, thinking at the time that it would be a good cover for him if and when he found the killers. Unbuttoning a shirt pocket, he fingered out the badge and said, "Wore this badge long enough to know I'll never be a marshal again."

"Heard you was taking over for Greenway until he healed up."

"On the other hand, Canada, we were planning on heading in for that celebration even before I took on this marshal's job. Perhaps the same thing would have happened . . . Jillian getting killed. Or me, for that matter." He forked another hunk of venison out of the frying pan resting on burning embers, and helped himself to more beans, then rocked back to settle against his saddle.

He went on. "No question they were after Pettigrew. But it was the way they opened up on innocent people that I can't tolerate. Once I get Tanner McKitrick in my gunsights, he's going down."

"Been hearing about how them McKitricks are riding a wide hell-roaring swath across Montana and other places." He sniffed the cooling air of early night. "Gonna be chilly again; but clear tomorrow for riding. Do you partake of alcohol, Mr. Lonigan?"

"Not one of my strong suits."

"Mine neither—but on nights such as this a drop or two in the belly sure starts a nice fire." He ambled over to his saddlebags and brought back a flask encased in a leather binding. "My own home brew." Tossing the rest of his coffee and some grounds out of his tin cup, Canada poured in a couple of fingers, and with one black-lignite eye lidding to show of his acceptance of Rain, he passed over the flask.

For a while they sipped from their cups, lost in private musings. Beyond the elevation protecting them from the prevailing northerly winds came the insistent hammering of a woodpecker at a tree. And there was just enough light for them to catch the bright yellowish tint of a goldfinch flitting overhead. Abruptly, the golden tints fell away from the western sky, and all at once a lot of stars seemed to appear.

"I've killed my share," Canada Reese suddenly drawled. "Got to me at first. Even though they was mostly Injuns. But closing into the '80's you'd think those killing days was over. What with towns springing up all over to damned near destroy the Great Plains. Well, us plainsmen had our day roaming from one end of the plains to the other. Then came the buffer hunters. Followed by gunslingers. Some call this an honorable profession,

Rain. The McKitricks . . . just plain murderers. We catch up with them, Mr. Lonigan, me and that old Sharps will back your play."

"Thanks, Canada . . . but, but are you sure about this?"

"Spoke on it, didn't I," he snapped. "Best be turning in. 'Cause now that we've got a trail to follow, come morning I expect to chase after it until starlight time."

Long after Canada Reese had hunkered into his bedroll, Rain took the pains to clean his weapons as he sat before the campfire. He had found since the death of his wife that turning in early was a memory-wracked ordeal, as he'd lie there remembering how it had been with Jillian. The more he pondered over it, the more Rain was coming to a decision to sell his spread, and it didn't make any difference where he went from there. But just to some place far enough away so there wouldn't be anything to remind him of the past.

He let the hammer down to have it slam onto an empty chamber of his sixgun, the metallic sound causing Canada's gelding to whicker nervously.

"They say a man changes after he's killed someone. For Rain Lonigan that's already happened."

Chapter Fifteen

On the afternoon of the second day out of Squaw Gap the vague trail left by the killers had been wiped out by a passing herd of Texas cattle. Northward dust could be seen paling the horizon. Slowly the plainsman and Rain Lonigan brought their broncs over a wide section of prairie gouged by the hooves of cattle and horses of the cowhands guiding them. For some unexplained reason the wind had ceased that awful and constant yowling, with just their low voices or creaking of saddle leather telling of their presence.

Canada Reese had told his saddle companion the trail they'd been following could have been made by cowpokes sent out to fetch cattle that often strayed out of the Badlands. And they were south of Wibaux and perhaps on land claimed by Huidekoper's Little Missouri Horse Company, going on to tell Rain that Baker, territorial Montana, lay beyond those low ridges to the southwest.

"Seems strange to be out here and not have to watch out for an Indian war party."

"Baker's a regular stop on the Fitz & Morehouse stagecoach line. Lively enough to make the McKitricks want to stop there. If not for supplies, Canada, just to get a copy of the *Billings Gazette*."

"Telling of how Johnston Pettigrew got gunned down. What do you suppose, the McKitricks got hired to do this?"

"That's about the only thing that makes sense to me."

"I was talking to Doc Barcome after this thing had happened," said Rain. "Said that from the way Pettigrew had reacted, up there on that speaker's stand, that he'd known Tanner McKitrick."

Hawking tobacco juice over his shoulder, Canada Reese retorted, "The law at Baker, Yarborough, should be able to fill in a lot of cracks."

Which proved to be the case when they rode into Baker just before last light and found Marshal Bull Yarborough holding court in Pehlan's Broken Bow saloon. An offer of a bottle of whiskey, and the fact the marshal and Reese were old acquaintances, enticed Yarborough back to a scarred table by a dusty window. This was the time of day a lot of those in here had just gotten off work, just to rehash the day's events though two poker games were in progress. Some free vittles, deer sausage, crackers, cheese, and a big crock holding bean soup, stood on a side table, which was seeing plenty of action.

One glance told anyone that Bull Yarborough was not a man to trifle with, as he seemed one solid mass of muscle packed on a towering six-five frame. The marshal wore shades of brown, and no handgun. A right hand twice the size of Rain's toyed with a shot glass. Yarborough had a habit of smiling quickly and often, his voice a double-octave baritone. After a couple of get-acquainted glasses of corn liquor, he responded to a question

143

from Canada Reese.

"If the McKitricks came through Baker, it would have been at night. But I could ask around."

"Rain here, is the law at Squaw Gap."

"The newspapers said it was a massacre."

"That about sums it up. Marshal Yarborough, we don't have much to go on. Only that they seemed to be after Johnston Pettigrew."

Again that smile. "Pettigrew has more enemies than ticks on a steer."

"Meaning someone hired the McKitricks to do this."

"Thinking back on it, Pettigrew got himself involved in some loansharking operation at . . . yup, Bozeman. But as usual, Pettigrew managed to pin the blame on others. I suppose that's the mark of a good politician."

"Bozeman's west a far piece," said Canada.

"Not far enough," responded Rain.

"You want to find out more, Lonigan, I suggest you stop at Billings and take a gander at some back issues of the *Gazette*."

"Now that word of this has gotten out," said Rain, "that the McKitricks did the killing, they just might hole up for a spell."

Yarborough said, "Meaning they'll keep to the back roads and out of the way cowtowns. Out here, as you know, there are a lot of towns where outlaws have settled in, sought honest work and such, married. Some of them could have ridden with the McKitricks in the past. But if I was you, gents, there's a place that is wide open and not that far away—Broadus. What you've got there is a saloon run by Dirty Jake Turley; and there's other places barely a dishonest cut about Dirty Jake's."

"Been through Broadus," commented Canada Reese as he eyed the side table and the brown crock of bean soup. "Wild, as you said, Bull."

"You said there were six of them."

"Seven, but one got killed."

"Even so," said Yarborough, "taking that many won't be easy. The McKitricks are gunhands, especially that Wade."

"Life is never easy," Rain said bitterly as Canada Reese shoved up and headed for the side table. "They killed my wife . . . and a few others."

"Seems to me the McKitricks are wanted men in Montana. It could be they'll be caught and made to stand trial here."

"I aim to either kill them or bring them back."

"You seem awful determined, Marshal Lonigan."

"I am."

"Just don't be blinded by it."

Later, Rain Lonigan thought about Yarborough's friendly words of warning in a room he shared with Reese at a local hostel. Across the room the even snores of Canada Reese were comforting, told him he wasn't alone in his quest for the McKitricks. Though two days of riding had worked out some of the kinks, and he felt more at ease, in this darkened room with just a few beads of light trickling past drawn curtains, he couldn't shake Jillian away. Nor, at the moment, did he want to. Someplace in the hotel he heard a door slam, then footsteps in the hallway, now silence.

"G'night," he finally mumbled after what seemed hours, to fall into a troubled sleep.

* * *

Back about fifteen years it was common to see Broaddus cattle roaming over what was later called Powder River County. When a town was established at a junction of two riverines, the Little Powder emptying murky waters into the Powder River, it was decided to name the place Broaddus, but a clerical error back in Washington City caused one D to be dropped from the name, and so it was Broadus that became the county seat. The cowtown hinged upon Northern Cheyenne country. Just south of Broadus along the Powder River, Crazy Horse and his Hunkpapas had a bloody skirmish against elements of the 7th Cavalry. Some of this was narrated to Rain Lonigan as he cast anxious eyes westward to the cowtown nodding under a simmering noonday sun.

"Looks peaceful enough."

"So does a wild hoss until you rile it up. Ghosted through here a few years back. Grown some."

"What does it have in the way of law?"

"Never stopped long enough to find out. Sure packed with saloons and such."

"Canada," Rain said upon dismounting and draping his reins over the hitching rack, "I've got a bad feeling about this place. No need to call upon the local law . . . as I figure we'll find out about the McKitricks in some saloon."

"Suits me."

"Shouldn't be any trouble finding Dirty Jake Turley's place."

"We could ask other places."

"We could. But if the McKitricks came through,

it was to hang low for a few days."

"Maybe they're still camped out at Dirty Jake's?"

"Only one way to find out."

To the few passersby, Rain and the plainsman were just a couple of drifters. In passing a cafe, Canada Reese hesitated, but when Rain kept on going, so did Reese but at a reluctant gait. He grumbled some around the wad of chewing tobacco, and held up when Rain paused to find out the location of Dirty Jake's saloon from a clerk stepping out of a dry goods store with a basket of tomatoes.

"You're looking for the Powder Saloon — up yonder on the right."

"Obliged," said Rain. "By the way, you wouldn't have noticed six men riding in about a week about . . . from the east?"

"Got all sorts passing through, mister."

"These men were outlaws. One of them would be a somber-clad gent having all the earmarks of a preacher . . ."

"Well, about a week ago, I guess, a bunch did ride in. Around sundown it was; just about when I got off work. Could have been them as they made tracks for Dirty Jake's."

When they were farther along the boardwalk, Rain said, "You were right about the McKitricks coming through here. I doubt if they're still around, Canada."

"But what if they are?"

"Then my first bullet is meant for that lying sky pilot."

"That being the case, no sense both of us showing up together. I'll sashay on ahead and see what I can find out." Canada Reese ducked under the hitch rack and untied his reins. "Give me a half hour. And you'd better fork over some dinero as I'm running short. I'll buy a bottle and pass it around to loosen a few tongues. Always worked before."

"Don't get careless in there." He handed Reese a half dozen silver dollars. He stepped to his horse and made a pretense of checking his saddle rigging as Canada Reese tied up his mount along the south wall of the Powder Saloon. When Reese moved around to the front of the long, two-story building and swung through the batwings, Rain brought his horse downstreet. He swung it in alongside Canada's.

Eying the small pole corral and barnlike building out behind the saloon, Rain meandered back there. He checked out the brands on three horses inside the corral; one brand was unknown to Rain, while the mouse-colored bronc was marked with the familiar Rafter Circle brand. He figured them to either be owned by those working at the saloon or cowhands in for a good time. In the building he found that it contained a lot of discarded junk and a buggy that was in good shape, and two more horses stabled there. One of the horses was big and chunky, but the other one held Rain's attention.

"The Diamond A—seems to me that brand is registered as being out of Wyoming?" The bronc, a rangy gray, lashed out with a hind leg at Rain as it slammed nervously into a stable wall.

The four other stalls were empty, though they

148

showed sign of recent use, a fact which stayed with Rain as he came outside and took in the outer staircase running up to the second floor landing. I'll bet, he mused, many an owlhooter has availed himself of that staircase when a lawman came calling, the last ones being those McKitricks. He would bet his ranch on that hard fact. But even as Rain walked back to the front boardwalk, he couldn't shake the presence of that Diamond A bronc out in the barn.

"Come on, try thinking like one of those McKitricks. It would be just like them to leave someone hanging back. Not a McKitrick though, but one of the other killers."

Upon entering the Powder Saloon he found it to be a bawdy, smoke-filled barroom. In a way it reminded him of the old Vagabond Saloon back at Sentinel Butte, with its yellow plastered walls marred by vague scrawlings, and by the yellowed-over windows and in corners plaster had rotted away to show the wood underneath. Since it was the middle of the day the overhead lamps were out. But he had little trouble singling out hardcases amongst a lot of others packing in to crowd the bar or try their luck at the games. The bar girls wore lacy red blouses, tight black skirts chopped off just below the knee and black mesh stockings; a jaded lot. He evaded an inviting smile from a girl old enough to have borne him as he sought the sanctity of the bar. He ordered a cold glass of beer from a bardog spiffed up in a white shirt and black bowtie, and whose black hair was slicked tight to the shape of his skull. Deftly he palmed Rain's silver dollar and pivoted to drop the coin in a cash drawer. For change Rain got a couple of quarters, and he said quietly, "Beer is damned expensive in here."

"The way we like it." The bardog's unfriendly eyes spun toward someone wanting his stein refilled.

With the glass in hand, Rain turned and began looking through the smoke and past those standing about for Canada Reese. After a while and off to the right he glimpsed the plainsman huddled at a table with a man wearing a checkered suit, the third man seated there clad in bib overalls and straw hat but with a gunbelt buckled around his waist, and also galoshes stained with dried manure. It seemed that Canada Reese was doing the bulk of the talking, though checkered suit would respond at times, and with bib overalls nodding in agreement. Once he caught Canada looking at him standing at the bar. Shortly thereafter the plainsman left those at a table with a smile as he shuffled up and headed toward the back door. To have Rain drain his glass and find the batwings again.

Reaching their horses at about the same time, Canada Reese said, "The McKitricks was here. But left two days ago."

"Did you find out where they were heading?"

"West is about all."

"At least," grimaced Rain, "you were right about them coming this way. If they stick to the main roads we won't be able to pick up their trail."

"Don't look now," muttered Canada Reese as he untied the reins, "but I just spotted someone ducking in behind that corral."

"And one on the roof!" warned Rain. Then the

150

sixgun was in his hand and swiveling up to the roof of the saloon. He pumped two slugs at a man holding a rifle while trying to control his bronc. The rifle sounded with a slug tugging at Rain's flapping vest before a slug from his gun brought the ambusher falling off the roof.

Canada Reese had gone into a crouch to exchange gunfire with another man holding out inside the corral. There hadn't been time for the plainsman to go for his Sharps, and he realized his handgun was no match for that Winchester, when suddenly he became aware of Rain Lonigan pounding past him crouched in the saddle. Upon spotting Rain, the other ambusher snapped off a wild shot as he broke across the corral. One leg suddenly went out from under him, and he pitched forward, losing his grip on the rifle, but managing to claw out his handgun.

"Drop it, damn you, or the next one blows out your heart!"

"Awright," he cried out at Rain Lonigan staring down at him from just outside the corral, "awright, hold your fire." Making a pretense of discarding his handgun, the hardcase suddenly brought it bearing toward the horseman, only to gasp in surprise when a slug took him full in the chest. "Damn . . . you busted my kneecap . . . now you . . ."

Rain slipped through the corral poles and closed in to kick the handgun away. "You were one of those who did the killings at Squaw Gap."

"Never been to . . . Squaw Gap . . ."

"I came upon you and two others playing pool."

"Yeah, I'll be damned . . . you're that marshal . . ."

"He's hit bad, Rain."

He glanced to his left at Canada Reese sitting his horse, and back to the wounded hardcase. "I want the McKitricks."

"Then go find them. All I want is a sawbones . . . damn, my kneecap . . ."

"What about the other one?"

"Breathed his last."

"You . . . I want the truth about where the McKitricks are heading!"

"Go to hell . . . marshal."

"You scummy bastards killed my wife," Rain lashed out. "So this is your last chance . . ."

The bluster went out of the hardcase's eyes, and he forgot about his chest wound and broken kneecap as he blurted out, "Awright . . . they . . . they're heading for Bozeman."

"Hey?" someone shouted, "they killed Larry Madden!"

"Over there . . . by the corral. Get 'em, boys!"

"Come on," shouted Canada Reese as he brought Rain's horse to the backside of the corral, and when Rain sprang into the saddle, he spurred his gelding back of the barn and toward some screening trees. Bullets spurted after Rain and Canada Reese urging their horses past the trees and into a coulee drifting northwesterly.

When, a couple of miles out of Broadus, there were no riders coming after them, Canada Reese slowed his horse to a walk and said, "Bozeman, he said."

"A long ride. But one I'm gonna make, Canada."

"That other hardcase was hit real bad. Doubt if he makes it through the night."

"Yeah," Rain muttered in bitter wonderment, "I just killed my first man . . . if you can call him that. You okay?"

"Nary a scratch."

They pressed on, and at Canada's urging, cut up north to find the main road. "Crosscountry is fine if you're out after game and such. As for what just happened, they don't know us from a lost tumbleweed."

"That hardcase made me out as being the marshal of Squaw Gap."

"Right now all he's worried about is getting to a sawbones. Suppose he does tell him who you are, Rain. The next thing they'll ask that hardcase is why the marshal of Squaw Gap was after him."

"I expect he won't talk at that, Canada." He threw the plainsman a concerned glance. "I hired you on to do some tracking. So if that hardcase wasn't lying about the McKitricks heading for Bozeman, you're free to call it quits."

"Back there at Broadus," muttered Canada, as he speared the other rider with an ambered stare, "that one hombre cutting down at us from the corral damn-near missed the tavern wall. While I noticed the other one up on that roof got a spur caught in some roof shingles otherwise he would have ventilated at least one of us. Meaning we lucked out. It won't be that way you catch up to the McKitricks by your lonesome. Not at all. You blink facing one of them, you're dogmeat. Besides, Mr. Lonigan, your innards are wracked with pain over what happened back at Squaw Gap. Maybe one of these cold nights you'll need someone to chew at."

"Maybe I will at that, Canada."

"Another thing. No sense us riding all that way to Bozeman as I figure the McKitricks are doing. We could angle up to Forsyth, catch a ride on one of them trains."

"That'll sure save us a lot of saddle sores." They were silent for a few miles, and then Rain slapped the ends of his reins lightly against the neck of his bronc. "You know, Canada, never thought I'd ever kill someone."

"The first time does eat at a man. For some killing comes easier; those are the gunslingers, I reckon. But consider what you did justful retribution. I'd do more than that if one of them harmed my woman . . . I'd be wearing a scalplock at my belt."

Chapter Sixteen

Livingston in territorial Montana was a long way from the Badlands and that killing day at Squaw Gap. But the McKitricks and Brent Wilmar still had to make it the rest of the way through Bozeman Pass. Hard riding had worn out their horses, and with some reluctance they'd paid out hard cash for fresh horses at Lodge Grass, these from a Crow running a small spread just outside that small Indian encampment. First they kill Custer and his troopers, Blaine McKitrick had retorted, now these Injuns take our money. After informing his brother that the Crows had fought on the side of the cavalry, Tanner McKitrick had insisted they keep on the move. To have them reach Livingston a couple of days later. There'd been this temptation to leave their horses and go on to Bozeman by train. But Wade McKitrick's spotting their pictures adorning the front page of a Billings newspaper brought them up well before sunup and moving out again.

Bozeman Pass, they were discovering, was a deep gorge staring up at sheer mountain ledges and high peaks, of the Bridger and Gallatin ranges. They were keeping to the old stagecoach road, which in some places had been worn away by creek water. A freight train chugging westward brought a scowl from Blaine McKitrick.

"I still think we should have got on a train. This damned mountain riding is pure hell on my backside."

Tanner McKitrick ignored the angry ramblings of his younger brother as he stared after the freight train lining back black smoke. He'd had his hair trimmed at Livingston and the beard shorn off, to reveal a few acne scars on his jawline as well as a scar caused by a knuckleduster. This made him look younger, though there was no hiding the patches of gray nor the brooding sarcasm in his eyes. Now he spoke what was on his mind.

"Wade, we've come a long way to get the rest of that money. Back to where a lot of folks know us."

"That money was deposited in a Bozeman bank under an assumed name. But you're right about all of us riding in there. Especially when we've been decorating the front pages of a lot of newspapers. We'll reach Bozeman around mid-afternoon. It's a big enough place so that if we mosey in alone nobody'll pay us any mind."

"Afterwards it might not be a bad idea to get some supplies and then cut out. South, this time, as Blaine suggested. Down into Old Mexico."

"You still want to pick up the money, Tanner? I could do it."

"Reason I shaved off this beard."

Tanner McKitrick took a long savoring pull

from a Mex cheroot. He brought the smoke deep into his lungs from where he stood under the covered arcade of the Plantation Hotel. He had always liked Bozeman, especially the way the mountains skirted around this large cattle town. Under a deep indigo sky he let his gaze descend along Hargrave Street to carpenters hammering roof boards into place on a new building. The street was crowded, and the few who glanced at him did so with incurious eyes. It was his feeling that Bozeman would be a good place to settle into, for there'd be hunting in the mountains, the rivers hereabouts swarming with trout.

About two hours ago they had ridden out of Bozeman Pass, to head north and ghost along the edges of the town. He had sent Blaine and Brent Wilmar in first; just a few minutes ago he'd spotted Wilmar taking his ease on a bench out in front of a saloon. He supposed Blaine was inside. Wade, despite Tanner McKitrick's objections, had also ridden in, and then to look up the owner of a local casino, and hoping the man could tell him where to find Frank Modahl. That was just like Wade when someone wronged him, the need to get even overriding his usually good judgment. He'd told Wade to be here around two-thirty, as the Gallatin County Bank closed a half-hour later.

"Knowing Wade," he muttered silently, worriedly, "he could be eyeballing me from a nearby saloon. He'll show; but dammit I wish he'd tend to the business at hand first."

Most of Tanner McKitrick's worry was for their dwindling cash supply. What they got today would help them a long way toward getting down into

Mexico. But along the way it would be business as usual, hitting a bank here or there, maybe a Wells Fargo office. Always keeping on the move with fresh horses under them and their saddlebags bulging with greenbacks. He couldn't fathom any other lifestyle. And grudgingly the gunhand had to admit he was getting old, getting tired of these long rides, letting himself brood on the cold fact the next bank job they pulled could see him going down. He was in Sheridan when a bank had been robbed, the two outlaws never making it to their horses, and later to have their bullet-riddled corpses placed in chairs out in front of an undertaker parlor for public viewing. So it wasn't getting killed that bothered him but being humiliated afterward. What he hadn't told his brothers was of this strong urge to open either a saloon in Texas or some casino in one of those Mexican border towns. Then Wade and Blaine, and other hardcases, would have a place to hide out when things got too hot for them in the territories.

He crossed over after a freight wagon had rumbled past, and nodded courteously at a rancher just ambling out of the bank. The bank lobby was ringed by a few teller cages and a low partition behind which clerks were working at desks. A wall clock told him it was a quarter until the hour. A teller glanced at Tanner McKitrick, then looked away.

"Could I help you."

The outlaw turned to smile at a middle-aged man pushing up from one of the desks, and McKitrick said, "You just might be able to. Name's John Conrad. Here to get some property of mine placed in one of your safety deposit boxes."

"Conrad, you say?"

A gloved hand slipped under the lapel of his black coat. It emerged holding a telegram, which Tanner McKitrick unfolded and handed to the bank official, who said, "This will do nicely." He opened a gate in the partition and went ahead of McKitrick, then he requested that the man he assumed to be John Conrad to have a seat in a small room. "Sorry, Mr. Conrad, but only bank employees are allowed access to the vault." He went away to return moments later with a green metal box. He placed this on the table before Tanner McKitrick, handed a key over, and with a fawning smile he closed the door upon leaving.

The box opened easily. But the expectant smile went away when Tanner McKitrick realized there was no money in the box, just a yellow envelope. "Damn, what's going on?" An angry hand lifted out the envelope. He tore it open.

He found the letter was addressed to his brother, Wade. And it went,

Mr. Wade McKitrick—

I place the blame of what happened before on Johnston Pettigrew. Too late did I realize that Pettigrew has absolutely no scruples. When this business matter ended between us only a few short months ago I was on the verge of ruination. So, in a desperate frame of mind, I came to only one conclusion, that Johnston Pettigrew had to die.

There were others Pettigrew had wronged. But what he did to me was a deeply grievous

159

act of an uncaring man, as he also wronged you, Mr. McKitrick, by sending the law after you and your brothers. Little did the people of Montana know this when they named Pettigrew as one of their delegates to Washington City. But the deed has been done, and so a man we hated is dead.

The notice of your arrival will be brought to my attention by one of my agents working for the bank. So to receive your due wages, Mr. McKitrick, it is necessary that on the evening of your arrival you come out to Hillside Cemetery, where the money will be handed over. Until then, I remain,

Farnsworth . . .

"So it was Farnsworth." He read the letter again, then he crumbled it up and thrust it into a pocket. And as Tanner McKitrick made his way out of the bank, he tried sorting out what he remembered about Lydel Farnsworth. A somewhat withdrawn man, a rancher liking to invest money in business ventures. But it was Ella Farnsworth who ruled the roost, to further recollect that time when he'd sought out Johnston Pettigrew at his suite in a prominent hotel here in Bozeman. The door to the suite had been left unlocked, allowing him access. A sliver of light coming from one of the bedrooms drew him over, where he glimpsed naked flesh and sensuous laughter, and silently he'd withdrawn. Now, pondering it over, the only answer he could come up with was Lydel Farnsworth finding out his wife had been involved with Pettigrew. Had to be this, since in his opinion

Farnsworth was a peaceable man.

Tanner McKitrick found a saloon, and had barely jackknifed onto a chair when one of his brothers sauntered in. He let Blaine order a bottle of whiskey, let his younger brother settle anxiously onto another chair before Tanner said, "There was no money."

"Damn, I knew . . ."

"Just this letter." He patted his coat pocket. "From Lydel Farnsworth."

"So it was him behind this."

"So it seems."

"No money means that dammit, we've got to go after Farnsworth."

"Simmer down," said Tanner McKitrick, as his eyes flicked to his brother Wade and Brent Wilmar shouldering through the door. He clicked his teeth together when a bartender brought over their whiskey and some shot glasses. Then he let the newcomers settle down at the table as he poured drinks around.

"You came out of that bank empty-handed."

"Not necessarily, Wade. It seems Lydel Farnsworth has been bankrolling this. Wants to meet us out by the local cemetery come sundown."

"With the money?"

"What he said in his letter."

"Well?"

"Only choice we've got."

"I don't like it."

"Blaine, it ain't up to you to like anything. Farnsworth knows that if he doesn't divvy up he's gonna take up permanent residence at that cemetery."

"Well," shrugged Wade McKitrick, "we've got a couple of hours to kill. And so far so good." His eyes flickered to the half-dozen customers idling in the saloon, whereupon he fixed a lazy smile on his face and tipped back his hat. "Feels good to have my backside resting in this chair instead of in that damned saddle. Meet him at this cemetery? You feel easy about that, Tanner?"

"I won't feel easy until we're heading south out of Montana. You and me'll go in while Will and our brother cover us. Now, Blaine, do you recollect what Farnsworth looks like?"

"Somewhat on the wiry side, Tanner. Somewhat shorter'n me . . . and is sporting that walrus mustache. And if it turns out to be Farnsworth?"

"I doubt if he'll try any funny stuff as I've got his letter."

"So, we've got everything covered," said Wade. "How's about some stud poker to pass the time."

The outskirts of Bozeman had edged out to Hillside Cemetery, a tidy chunk of land occupying a hillock just short of where a creek meandered out of the mountains to the east. Troubling Tanner McKitrick were the higher slopes just beyond the cemetery, with patches of meadow hemmed in by firs. There were more trees on the lower ground to the west and buildings, and a road that had been built up as it passed through marshy ground. His gaze returned through the uncertain light still holding back shadows to the cemetery entrance, an opening in a low stone wall and an overhead portico made from shaped iron.

162

"I don't like it."

"You think it might be a trap?"

"Pettigrew's dead. The same could happen to us. Blaine, you and Will out through those trees and work your way around to the north to higher ground. Cover us when we go in."

"Be pitch dark soon, Wade."

"Won't be long before the moon shows."

"I hope so," grumbled Blaine McKitrick as he reined off to the left and jogged his horse away, with Wilmar jogging a little faster to catch up.

Wade McKitrick speculated, "Maybe Farnsworth is waiting for us to ride in first."

"We'll let him make the first move," Tanner said patiently. "He don't pay up, we'll take out both Farnsworth and his missus." Then he reached out to touch Wade's arm when a buggy appeared on one of the lanes running out from the nearby streets of Bozeman. One man sat on the buggy seat sawing at the reins, and even when the buggy came closer they couldn't make out if it was Lydel Farnsworth.

When the buggy passed into the cemetery and drew up under an elm tree, Wade said, "I figure it's him."

"Could be Farnsworth," he said cagily, and with a pondering glance taking his eyes beyond the cemetery. "By now they should be in place." He brought a spur nudging into the underbelly of his bronc, but even as Tanner McKitrick rode along-side his brother toward their meeting with Lydel Farnsworth, he kept glancing about and twisting around to try to pierce beyond the screening trees and buildings. Riding with him went a certain

163

wariness as of a lobo wolf finally heading in to pick a trap clean.

At the entrance to the cemetery Wade McKitrick said, while trying to make out the features of the man waiting for them by the buggy, "It sure enough looks like Farnsworth. What say you keep watch here whilst I do the palavering." His right hand grasped the butt of the Peacemaker and eased it out of the holster, shoved it back again, the touch of his weapon easing some of his tension. Could be, he mused, some of Tanner's skittishness is rubbing off on me. Then he walked his bronc through the gateway and veered leftward. Only to have Lydel Farnsworth suddenly duck behind the buggy and seemingly draw a weapon.

"It's a trap!" he shouted as guns began opening up from inside the cemetery, and as Wade McKitrick suddenly realized ambushers had been hiding behind tombstones.

From the south men on horseback swept in to have Tanner McKitrick draw up short on his reins and swing his rearing bronc around, and even as he went for his handgun, he knew they didn't have a chance.

"Drop that weapon!" barked one of the horsemen.

"Throw your weapon away, Wade," Tanner yelled at his brother, even as he tossed his own gun away and raised his arms. From the north there came the rattling of more gunfire, a brief firefight that caused the hardcases' eyes to narrow worriedly. Being something of a hothead, Blaine, he realized, would try to gun his way out, and he hoped that his brother had done just that.

Tanner McKitrick was brought into the cemetery, where those who'd been lurking inside its dark confines had lighted torches. In their flickering glare he spotted the man who'd driven the buggy, and he said, "Farnsworth is more of a coward than I realized."

One of the riders said, "Harsh words for someone as cowardly as you, McKitrick."

"Well, if it isn't the esteemed sheriff of Bozeman."

"You were lucky to get away before," Sheriff Toby Springer lashed out. "By rights I should have my men hang you from that tree. For what you did back at Squaw Gap."

"You've got no proof on that."

"Shut the hell up, McKitrick, before I change my mind about not hanging you right here and now. So you wondered why Lydel Farnsworth didn't show. Bring both of them over here." The sheriff rode deeper into the cemetery as did the other riders, and men on foot holding weapons and torches, and then to come sidling up to a newer mound of dirt. "There's the reason."

Scrawled on the tombstone Tanner and his brother stared at was the name Lydel Farnsworth, the years of his life etched below that, and other decorative words. If not Farnsworth, wondered Tanner McKitrick, then who was behind this murder plot? Johnston Pettigrew collected enemies like others took to saving stamps or old pictures. There were others locally who'd lost money they had invested in this loansharking scheme. There were the four men Tanner and his brothers had gunned down over their refusal to keep up their payments. Men such as this had a lot of friends and relatives hereabouts. But it would take someone with considerable money to bankroll Wade's breakout from that prison, then to deposit more money over at Deadwood as a down payment on killing Johnston Pettigrew.

"But to hell with that," Tanner McKitrick muttered silently. "We were damn fools for coming back here." Then bitter anger stoned his face when one of the sheriff's deputies clapped a pair of handcuffs on his wrists.

"They're bringing in the others."

"Damn them," Wade McKitrick muttered as a bunch of riders came in bringing the bodies of Blaine and Brent Wilmar draped over their horses.

"Easy," said Tanner to his brother. "We know Blaine was always hotheaded. We're still alive . . . unless they decide to finish us off out here."

When the new arrivals rode in among the tombstones and up to men holding lighted torches, one of the horsemen urged his bronc under a screening elm and broke out laughing, to have him say derisively, "It was me that killed your brother."

"Frank Modahl, damn your black soul to hell!" Wade McKitrick spurred his horse toward the man who'd helped break him out of that territorial prison down in Wyoming. But he never quite got there as Sheriff Toby Springer swung the butt of his rifle out to catch Wade McKitrick in the side of the face. He fell, barely missing the lashing hoofs of his horse, which only served to make Frank Modahl's grin widen.

"We hang 'em here?"

"Nope, Modahl, they're my prisoners."

166

"Yeah, so you say." Frank Modahl reined around to have three other men break away and ride after him. Clearing the cemetery, he muttered, "At least we got two of them. You boys head over to Callahan's Bar; I'll join you later."

"Gonna see her?"

"She'll raise holy hell we didn't kill all of them," said the hardcase as he rode away.

A fifteen minute ride through the dark streets of Bozeman ended when Frank Modahl veered into a long curling lane and to come upon a large, two-story brick house. Tying up, he stood there for a moment while gazing at light pouring out of the lower windows, caught a glimpse of one of the servants going about some chore, and had this thought, Ella's sure enough a sassy bitch. Cold-blooded as hell, an' about as trusting as a rattler. A reluctant stride brought him to the front door, and he entered without bothering to knock. As he'd expected, he found Ella Farnsworth waiting anxiously in a study just off the spacious dining room, with a glass of wine at her elbow and a deck of cards spread out in a game of solitaire. She had on a slithery black velvet gown, with him sensing that was all she had on, and maybe slippers on her feet. Closer, he could make out the rising swell of her full breasts.

"We got two of them."

"I expected more," she snapped.

"The sheriff is taking Wade and Tanner McKitrick over to his jail."

Ella Farnsworth threw down the cards she'd been holding, rose to move over to a window and gaze at downtown Bozeman. "I don't like this."

167

"When I got back to the cemetery, they were gathered around your husband's grave."

"At least now they know Lydel is dead. This whole thing, Frank, leaving that letter in that safety deposit box, well, I just hope the sheriff doesn't turn on us. Besides you, he's the only one who knows I had you break Wade McKitrick out of prison."

"I reckon that sooner or later he'll tie you to what happened at Squaw Gap. That happens, Ella, Springer'll be taking blackmail money from you the rest of your natural days."

"Are you saying I should have the sheriff taken care of?"

Sweeping his Stetson from his head, Frank Modahl tossed it onto an overstuffed chair and came in behind her. Then he spun Ella around, wrapped an arm around her and brought his lips down hard upon hers. She tried pulling away, only to have his arm tighten as Modahl said, "Damn, you're a sassy bitch."

"No, Frank, damn you."

He grabbed her hair and lifted her head to gaze into her eyes flashing anger and just a shade of fear. "I did your dirty work. That was a long, dusty ride down into Wyoming. Tonight I took out two men for you. And I expect you'll want me to kill the other McKitricks. I expect I'll do it. But dammit, woman, not just for more money." His eyes going crazy with his need for her, he picked Ella Farnsworth up and spun toward one of the doors.

"Yes, Frank," she hissed as her body responded to his rough arms, "Yes, yes . . . I need you."

Then an arm encircled his thick neck and demanding lips found his weathered face as he carried Ella Farnsworth into a downstairs bedroom.

Chapter Seventeen

Arriving on an afternoon train, Rain Lonigan had just stepped down onto the depot platform carrying his saddle and warbag when a newsboy held up a newspaper and cried out, "Read all about it! Two men die in gunfight! McKitrick brothers captured!"

He crossed to the newsboy standing by one of the open depot doors and motioned for a newspaper as he managed to find a nickel in a pocket of his worn Levis. He scanned the front page as Canada Reese came over, and Rain said bitterly, "Blaine McKitrick is dead."

"The other brothers in jail."

"According to this story, Canada, the McKitricks will stand trial here in Bozeman. And for murder."

"Where they hang is all one and the same."

"Not to me it isn't," Rain said curtly. "What they did back in Squaw Gap went beyond murder." He bent to pick up his saddle, slung it over his back and set out with Canada Reese to his left.

"You may want them McKitricks to take back, Rain, but as I remember you quit packing a badge."

"Maybe so, Canada, but I brought one along. And it could be that's all I'll need to have the McKitricks turned over to me. That'll have to wait until tomorrow."

"Suits me. These old bones have been telling me for the last couple of days I need a hot bath and just maybe a feather bed. But that bed after I've got me some hot food and just a drop of the hard liquor."

"Thanks, Canada, for coming this far. Here we were all braced for a shootout. In a way I'm kind of glad we don't have to face their guns."

"Only the damnable foolhardy want to go up against gunfighters such as the McKitricks. Though I know, Rain, you would have faced up to them."

"That hotel will do." Rain Lonigan eased through the open door and went past a narrow staircase to receive a cordial smile from a woman standing behind a counter in the small lobby. Red checkered wallpaper tried but failed to make the lobby appear larger, and in places it was faded and cracked. "Ma'am, I don't know how long we'll be here."

"No matter. There's one room with two beds in it; clean towels are extra."

"Fine," said Rain in a tired voice, and as he scrawled his name on the register book. "Any stores still open?"

"It's only half past four, Mister . . . Lonigan. Most don't close until six. A dollar a day, in advance."

Rain paid for both of them, and he said, "Go ahead, Canada, you wash up first. I'm going to mosey out and get a new shirt and some socks." He went up the staircase behind Canada Reese and the desk clerk, the woman opening the last door on the right.

"Overlooks Sterling Street," she said. "Have a nice stay."

"That the bathroom just across the hall?"

"It is, and there's plenty of hot water. But, mind you, gents, try not to make a mess." A smile managed to work its way out between her pursed lips as she hurried down the hallway.

Rain Lonigan left, after depositing his gear on one of the beds. Out in front of the hotel, a storefront just upstreet brought him toward it, and with the sun coming at his back. The city was larger than he expected, and the many brick buildings strung along the street told Rain it was here to stay. Still scattered among the newer brick buildings were sheds, wooden buildings, a few empty lots. This was more a railroad than cowtown, even though a large scattering of horses were moving along the street or idling in front of business places, and there were the usual number of cowhands and ranchers. He went into a large mercantile store and found some shirts amid a plentiful supply of men's clothing. He picked out a blue cotton shirt that seemed to be about the right size as a clerk came over to inquire, "Will there be anything else, sir?"

While in the process of selecting a shirt, he couldn't help overhearing a conversation going on between three gents standing by one of the counters, the meat of it about the McKitrick brothers. "Is this just talk," Rain asked the clerk, "or are folks hereabouts thinking of getting up a lynching party?"

"That was all the talk at Lindahl's Cafe this morning. As you know, they were driven out of Bozeman last fall after some killings. Now what just happened in Squaw Gap has been in all the newspapers. I'd venture to say, sir, there isn't going to be any trial."

"Who has jurisdiction over the prisoners?"

"Sheriff Springer arrested them."

"I expect the U.S. marshal has his office over at the courthouse."

"Yes, it's there."

"Just wondering," said Rain as he paid for the shirt, and upon leaving, went back to the hotel and up to the room he shared with Canada Reese.

"That big brass tub sure hit the spot," said Reese. "While you're in there I'm gonna mosey down and do some palavering with that desk clerk."

"I thought you'd sworn off women . . ."

"Only squaws . . . but that could change too under different conditions." With one eye lidding in what passed for a wink Canada Reese ambled out of the room.

In a room across the hall Rain shed his clothes to reveal a body more leaned than it had been about a month ago. Now he seemed all muscles and sinew, with some new lines showing around his eyes and forehead, the eyes of Rain Lonigan as he settled into the large tub bitterly alert, tinted with sadness. After a while the hot soapy water relaxed trail-weary muscles, and made him feel drowsy. The McKitricks, he mused, have no

173

friends anyplace. But what brought them here? It doesn't make any sense them coming back to a town where they're wanted for murder. But on the other hand, those newspapers I've been reading tell that Johnston Pettigrew came from around these parts. So there's got to be a connection. Which I might find out from another lawman.

When Rain came down into the lobby, there was no sign of Canada Reese, and he said to the woman clerk, "You don't happen to know where Mr. Reese went?"

"Well," she answered as her face reddened, "Canada did ask if there were any saloons nearby . . . and I told him there was Finnegan's Ale House. Was . . . was Canada really a plainsman?"

"Among other things," smiled Rain, and with the star-shaped rowels of his spurs jangling when he headed for the open door.

Finnegan's Ale House proved to be just a saloon, but bigger than most with its overhanging balconies and a back stage where two men in blackface were spieling out a spirited rendition of the minstrel song, "Green Grow The Lilacs." A few smiles were on some engaged in games of chance, while at the long bar boots were tapping against the low brass railing. He had little trouble spotting Canada Reese hunched at a table just past one of the roulette wheels, and he went there. As Rain settled onto an empty chair, a barmaid laid a hand on his shoulder and asked, "What'll you have, handsome?"

Canada said, "They've sure got a fine assortment of Irish whiskey; stuff's savory as all getout."

"Some Irish whiskey, then, and a glass of beer."

"This time I'm buying," said Canada, to the clink of a couple of silver dollars hitting the table top. "Rain, this is Claude Enright, a sort of local historian and oldtime rancher."

"Over the hill rancher," responded Enright as he reached out a big and weathered hand to shake Rain's. There was a look of competence about the older man, and he had a graying walrus mustache below a hatchet nose and shaggy eyebrows. The cattleman's hat sat squarely on his head, the dark brown leather coat hanging open over a starched white shirt. There was a turquoise clasp in the string tie.

"We were discussing the recent spate of events here in Bozeman."

"Yes," said Enright, "though it didn't surprise me any too much when I heard that Johnston Pettigrew had been gunned down. A sorrowful thing, gentlemen, to happen to anybody. I was telling Canada"—he sipped from his shot glass—"that I was one of those who'd invested money with Pettigrew. Not all that much."

"Could you elaborate on that?"

With his words evenly spaced out, and in a raspy baritone, the rancher told of how Pettigrew had come in to start a moneylending business, and that he also dealt in stocks and bonds. "Somehow the interest he charged began escalating . . . damned absurd rates. Next thing we know he's brought in some hired guns to back his play."

"The McKitricks," said Rain. "Tell me, Mr. Enright, why would the McKitricks come back here?"

"Awful damned stupid of them. But it could be someone from here paid them to kill Johnston Pettigrew."

"That's about the only thing making sense out of this. But whoever did bankroll the McKitricks is just as guilty of murder."

"You seem like an angry young man, Mr. Lonigan."

Canada Reese said quietly, "Rain's wife was one of those who got killed back at Squaw Gap."

"I'm sorry to hear that," said the rancher. "Awful sorry. You have my condolences, Mr. Lonigan."

Nodding as the barmaid came back with the drinks he'd ordered, and a first round for his table companions, Rain said, "What about this lynch talk?"

"You'll hear of it here . . . and in every bar in Bozeman." Claude Enright grimaced as he stared at Rain. "I believe in observing the letter of the law. That this town must go by due process if it is to survive. Certainly the McKitricks deserve to be taken out and hung, pronto. But it'll be a sorry day for us. Speaking of stirring up folks hereabouts, I was downstreet a bit ago, at the Rainbow Saloon, as a matter of fact . . . anyway, there was this stranger in there and some with him inflaming others in there."

"About breaking the McKitricks out of jail and hanging them . . ."

"Yup, that's about it. Found out the one doing the most talking was a gent named Frank Modahl.

Had this hard look about him. Seems to me too, Mr. Lonigan, I saw him before . . . out by some-one's house . . . but it was kind of dark and I couldn't be all that certain."

"Perhaps the home of the person behind this?"

"Well, that could be. And sorry to rush away, gentlemen, but the missus should be about done over at the hairdressers. Take care now, and again, Mr. Lonigan, my condolences. Somehow . . . somehow I get the feeling you've been chasing after those killers. Well, that's none of my busi-ness. Good evening."

As the rancher ambled out of the saloon, Rain said pensively, "He didn't tell us all he knows."

"Seemed square enough to me."

"Yup, be a man to ride the trail with. You hun-gry?"

"Does a coyote love rabbit. That door to the left yonder leads into a dining room; been told the vit-tles are downright pleasing. Since I bought the drinks, the same goes for supper."

Rain Lonigan had taken to heart the sage advice he'd gleaned from Canada Reese around their lonely campfires, one piece of this being that in new territory a man had to get the lay of things. Upon arising this morning, Canada had struck off to find out what he could in the saloons. For Rain it was this short jaunt over to the newspaper of-fice, where he began poring over back issues of the *Bozeman Daily News*. He'd gone back nearly a year when the front pages began telling of the misdeeds of Johnston Pettigrew and his hired guns. But at the moment Rain was pondering over another copy of the newspaper in which the blame for all that had happened seemed to point to a local rancher, a Lydel Farnsworth.

"Somehow Pettigrew was smart enough to wiggle out of this. Otherwise folks up around here and over at Butte wouldn't have voted for the man. Maybe it only points out to what a smooth operator Pettigrew was. But what now?"

He went outside into a warm summery morning, weighing all that he'd just learned, and somehow trying to use a lawman's logic in this. It had come to Rain along the way—or perhaps this was some more of Canada Reese's sage words striking home—that he would have, at least for the here and now, to cast aside his deep anger, to replace this with clear thinking much like the unblemished blue dome overhead. The city jail, he had been told, lay farther east along the main drag, but closer was the courthouse and the domain of U.S. Marshal T. Hartwig. His chief reason for going there would be to find out if he needed extradition papers in order to have the McKitricks turned over to him. And perhaps he could find out the names of others who had bankrolled Johnston Pettigrew.

"So, Mr. Lonigan, Squaw Gap is a far piece from here."

"It is, Marshal Hartwig."

"Coffee?"

"Sure could use a cup."

"How do you like being a town marshal?"

Upon arriving at the courthouse, Rain had

178

veered off into a quiet corridor and pinned the marshal's badge to his shirt, and though he had felt out of sorts doing so, the moment passed when he thought about Jillian and the others who had died under the guns of the McKitricks and their accomplices. Somehow wearing the badge had steeled this wavering notion that a lynching would serve justice just as well as a jury trial.

"Until the McKitricks showed up it was a pretty quiet job."

"Read about it, Marshal Lonigan." He handed Rain a cup, and then he settled down behind his desk. Hartwig was leaned out and flint-eyed, with crow's-feet edging away from them, and with a starred badge pinned to his leather vest. "For certain the McKitricks will hang for what they did back there. But it seems the hanging will take place here."

"Under the circumstances I would think the McKitricks should be turned over to your office."

"They were arrested by Sheriff Toby Springer. This means my office is just one of the spectators. But it did rile me at the time Sheriff Springer knowing they would show up here, I mean, Lonigan, the sheriff not sharing that information."

"What you're saying, Marshal Hartwig, is that he was tipped off about the McKitricks showing up."

"My guess. But by whom?" He opened a small glass jar, scooped out a couple of sugar cubes and let them plop into his coffee cup. Stirring his coffee with a spoon, he added, "Springer is pretty thick with the local money men."

179

"Did you ever hear of a hardcase calling himself Modahl . . . Frank Modahl? Maybe have wanteds on him?"

"Offhand the name doesn't ring a bell. Any particular reason for asking?"

Rain set his cup down on the desk and shoved to his feet. "About all I know about Modahl is that he's behind a lot of this lynch talk."

"Hell, marshal, so's the rest of the town. Obliged for your coming in. I figure you'll be paying the sheriff a visit. Just warning you that Sheriff Springer gets awful cantankerous at times. He won't look too kindly to your wanting to have the McKitricks extradited back to Dakotaland. But good luck, Lonigan." Hartwig donned his hat and came around the desk. Then he walked with Lonigan out of a side entrance, and to have U.S. Marshal T. Hartwig nod toward a carriage house just back of the courthouse.

"Lonigan, if you are able to wrangle this, maybe you'll have to transport those killers back in something like that new marshal's wagon of mine."

Rain moved with the marshal so they had a closer view of the vehicle in question parked behind an open door. Constructed on lines similar to a stagecoach, the wagon was painted a coal black, it had small barred windows and a high driver's seat. The only door opened from the rear, and it was made to be pulled by four horses. "Bet that thing cost a lot of money."

"Some. Just got delivered here. Well, Marshal Lonigan, I've a meeting to attend. But drop in if I could be of any help."

180

Unlike the pleasant cordiality of the U.S. marshal, the sheriff of Gallatin County viewed with disdainful suspicion the badge worn by Rain Lonigan. A deputy, standing by one of the gun racks, threw Rain one of those fawning smiles as much to say he agreed with the sheriff. Which caused Rain to repeat his request that he be allowed to see the McKitricks.

"Squaw Gap, you say."

"Dakota Territory. I expect you know about what happened there."

"Everyone knows about that. Sorry, Lonigan was it? . . . but no dice about seeing my prisoners."

"My wife," Rain said icily, "was one of those who got gunned down. I came here as one lawman requesting the help of another. I came here, Sheriff Springer, with the intentions of bringing the McKitricks back to stand trial."

"Very well, Lonigan, you can see them."

Rain began unbuckling his gunbelt.

"But there's no way the McKitricks will leave Bozeman."

With a bitter smile for the sheriff, Rain dropped his gunbelt on the man's desk, then he went over and waited until the deputy had opened the barred door leading into the cell block. Upon entering, the door was locked again behind Rain as the deputy said curtly, "The McKitricks are our only prisoners. You've got five minutes."

"That'll have to do."

And as Rain moved along the uneven brick

floor, he could see one of the McKitricks pushing up from a low cot. This was Wade McKitrick, who waited until Rain came close to the cell door before he spoke.

"You sure as hell don't look like no lawyer. So I suppose you're the undertaker."

Tanner McKitrick, looking up from where he sat on his bunk, framed a tentative smile. "He's that lawman from Squaw Gap. Fancy seeing you out here, Lonigan."

Rain managed to choke down his anger when he gazed back at the bogus preacher. He said coldly, "What from I've been hearing, there won't be any trial."

"We know they're fixing to drag us out of here and hang us," replied Tanner McKitrick. "Those three deputies of Springer's taunt us about that every time they come in here. I suppose you'll be part of the lynching mob."

"The way I feel about what you did back there, McKitrick, I could be one of them all right. I came here hoping to get some answers."

"As to why we killed Pettigrew," jeered Wade McKitrick.

"That'll do for starters. And why you came back to a place where you were wanted for murder. I suspect to see the man who hired you to kill Johnston Pettigrew."

"Go to hell, Lonigan!"

"Easy, Wade," said his brother as he rose to step up to the closed cell door. He cast Rain Lonigan a probing look. "So far they haven't even allowed us to hire a lawyer, much less see one. Yes, Lonigan,

182

what you just said pretty much sums this up. We came back expecting to get paid. Only thing is, when I got to that bank there was just this letter telling me to head out to Hillside Cemetery. But instead of Farnsworth being there, it was the sheriff and his posse. Next thing we know we were staring down at Lydel Farnsworth's grave. Meaning, Lonigan, we don't know who hired us."

Rain could sense that the outlaw hadn't been lying, and then he mulled over what that rancher had told him over at Finnegan's Ale House, and he said, "Does the name Modahl mean anything to you?"

"Modahl," Wade blurted out, "was one of those out at the cemetery. The backshooting bastard killed Blaine . . . and Wilmar."

"Frank Modahl was one of those who helped Wade escape from that work gang down in Wyoming."

"Modahl is also the one behind most of this lynch talk," said Rain.

"You come here to watch us hang or for another reason, Lonigan? Maybe try to have us brought back to Squaw Gap?"

"That's why I'm here. I figure it'll either happen tonight . . . or in the next day or two, them breaking in here." Rain heard a key turning in the lock of the cellblock door. "I get the feeling the sheriff is in on this . . . that he knows who hired you to kill Pettigrew. He's against my taking you back to stand trial. So all I've got to go on is latching onto Frank Modahl, an' hoping he'll take me to the person he's working for."

"It could be Farnsworth's wife, Ella," Tanner McKitrick said quickly. "Pettigrew had been sparking her before he cut out of here. I'll bet she's the one." But his last desperate words were spoken to the back of Rain Lonigan moving up the narrow corridor.

Only when the cellblock door clanged shut again, did Tanner McKitrick turn to look at his brother. "Never expected Lonigan to show up."

Wade said jeeringly, "As I recall he wasn't much of a lawman."

"But he could be our salvation. Lonigan just might bust us out of here to save us from that lynch mob."

"That's right, Reverend Beecher, preach me one of them soul-saving sermons."

"We get out on that eastbound trail someplace, one miscue by Lonigan and he's dead."

"Amen, brother."

Chapter Eighteen

Around nine that evening Frank Modahl picked up his chips and heaved out of the chair. He ambled over to the cashier's cage, and after cashing in his chips, the hardcase left the gaming casino and sought the boardwalk. At the first corner he swung to the south and at the next, he eased deeper into shadows cast by a building, waited there for a few moments to make certain he wasn't being followed.

When he set out again, Frank Modahl had no idea that the plainsman, Canada Reese, and the former marshal of Squaw Gap were ghosting along his backtrail. So he plodded on, taking a zigzag course through quieter streets until he moved up a walkway being watched over by rustling trees. The horse tied out front of the big rambling house he recognized as belonging to Sheriff Toby Springer. At the front door he didn't hesitate but rambled on in, with an arrogant set to his face which softened some when he entered the study and gazed at Ella Farnsworth.

"You're late," she said nervously.

"Not all that much. Now why all the fuss about having this meeting?"

"Because," responded Ella, "a lawman from the Badlands showed up today."

"I made the mistake of letting Marshal Lonigan have a few minutes alone with the McKitricks."

"They don't know about Ella being involved in this."

"What you are dealing with, Frank," Springer retorted, "are desperate men. They'd make a deal with the devil if they figured it would get them out of my jail. So we've got to do it tonight, hang them."

"Should have done it out at that cemetery. So what do you have in mind?"

"I'll keep a couple of my deputies watching over the jail until say, around midnight. The town should be quieted down by then. After my deputies cut out, it'll be a simple matter for you and your men to move in and take care of the McKitricks. I've got some hanging ropes in my saddlebags."

"Sounds good," said Modahl. "Ella, you agree with that?"

"Just do it," she said tautly, and knowing that Modahl was teasing her, and that once he'd help hang those outlaws, Frank Modahl would come back to share her bedroom. But with the McKitricks out of the way, Modahl's usefulness would be over. So when he returned tonight instead of sharing her bed, the hardcase would be killed by the sheriff, and Modahl's body taken away, never to be found again. Despite her worried mood of the moment, the thought pleased Ella Farnsworth. For she loathed Modahl's crude mannerisms, and the way he had forced himself upon her.

"No sense me hanging around," remarked Springer.

"Just make sure your deputies are out of that jail," Frank Modahl waited until the sheriff had left, then he swaggered over to Ella standing by a corner bar. "Tonight, honeysuckle, after I do your dirty business for you, I'll be back. Or maybe there's time now . . ."

"First thing, Frank, Springer's out by his horse waiting to give you those hanging ropes. Then you don't have all that much time to get your men together and go over what you have to do."

"Reckon you're right," he said sullenly. "But Modahl'll be back . . . and with a big hankering for some easy loving."

Out by one of the corner windows looking into the study, Rain Lonigan had crouched lower when the sheriff had moved outside and gone over to his horse. He reached out and touched Canada's shoulder. "Well, we heard enough to know the McKitricks are as good as dead. Here comes Modahl."

Canada whispered back, "At least we've got a couple of hours to figure out what to do."

Now they watched the sheriff riding away, and Frank Modahl trudging after with the coiled ropes in one hand. They eased along the wall into a deeper blackness, from there loped across the wide expanse of lawn to sheltering trees.

"I've been mulling this over," said Rain, "about breaking the McKitricks out of jail. Before it would have meant pistol-whipping a deputy or

187

two. With nobody watching the prisoners, all we have to do, Canada, is move in before Modahl's bullyboys."

"And afterward? Out of jail them McKitricks can be dangerous as a bull going after a cow in heat."

"I was shown something this afternoon that would solve a lot of our problems. What we'll need are four horses to pull a U.S. marshal's wagon."

"Now what in tarnation is a marshal's wagon?"

"I figure a rolling jailhouse, Canada."

"Whatever. As for getting hosses, as late as it is, all of the livery stables are battened down for the night. But . . . nothing like playing this Injun style and helping ourselves to what we need. A marshal's wagon, that be U.S. government property . . ."

"That it be. Being a taxpayer, Canada, I figure Uncle Sam owes me a rebate of some kind."

"What about that woman back there, do you think she's behind all of this?"

"The way I see it," Rain said somberly. "But right now there's nothing I can do about her. Why she wants them dead is that the McKitricks can tie her to what happened at Squaw Gap. They get lynched, Canada, we might as well head back to the Badlands. Where we'll be heading once we get the McKitricks into that marshal's wagon."

"A long trip."

"I was pondering on this, that once we clear Bozeman Pass and reach Livingston, we can go the rest of the way by train."

"For now, let's consider getting them hosses. There's a livery stable; shuttered up though." He followed Rain over to the back door, which they managed to swing ajar. A quick search inside revealed only one horse tethered in a stall.

"As I recollect," drawled Canada, "over on the next street there's this livery stable; horses stabled there are used by this stagecoach outfit. Meaning there'll be harnesses."

Rain Lonigan's luck was holding when they arrived at the stable to find that the hostler had left for the night. Once they'd secured entrance, by lanternlight they set about throwing harnesses on four horses, which were skittish at first, but soothing words from Canada brought them back to eating hay. They brought the horses out the back door and by back streets in the direction of the courthouse.

"We shouldn't have any trouble getting the marshal's wagon out of that carriage house, Canada. Then we'll go to our hotel and get our gear. We'll head over and ease our rig in behind the jail or close enough to watch for them deputies pulling out."

The carriage house, as Rain had anticipated, was as he'd seen it last, the door standing ajar to reveal the wagon they sought. But he opened the door farther to let moonlight spill in as Canada brought one pair of horses stepping over the wagon tongue, and with Rain handling the other pair. Once the traces were attached to the doubletrees, the reins were passed up to Canada Reese just getting up onto the high seat.

"Got this new smell to it," he said, "but sure enough a strange-looking rig." Once Rain had clambered up, he reined the horses out of the carriage house and away from Bozeman's slumbering courthouse.

Around midnight by Rain Lonigan's reckonings a deputy poked his head out of the back door and surveyed the approaches to the jail. But when the deputy turned to go back inside he left the door standing partly open, to which Rain said, "Seems the sheriff did sell out to that Ella Farnsworth."

"There the pair of them go out the front door," said Canada Reese, from where he stood by the front team of horses to calm them. He patted the near horse before releasing his grip on the halter chain. The horses were tied up to a tree a few yards away from a storage shed across the alleyway from the jail.

Loping away from the marshal's wagon and across the alley, Rain slipped inside to find himself in a small room cluttered with supplies, guns resting in wall racks, and varying leg and wrist irons hanging from wall pegs. He told Canada to pick out some irons as the next room proved to be the sheriff's office, the door to the cellblock standing open, the key for this door and the cells reflecting dull lamplight. He reached for the keys in passing and hurried back along the narrow corridor. Rain's boots resounding on the brick floor brought Tanner McKitrick up from his bunk.

Rain thrust one of the keys into the key opening

190

as he said, "It's me, that marshal from Squaw Gap. Any minute now a lynch mob is gonna bust in here."

"How do we know that?"

"For one thing, McKitrick, the deputies skedaddled out of here about five minutes ago. For another, me and Canada followed Frank Modahl over to Lydel Farnsworth's house. Eavesdropped enough to know it was Farnsworth's widow who hired you boys to kill Pettigrew. Now the widow Farnsworth wants you dead."

"So it was her!" said Tanner McKitrick. "Yeah, she wants us dead so's we can't bear witness to her hiring us."

"Now you know," said Rain as he unlocked the cell door and palmed his sixgun, as did Canada.

The plainsman tossed the irons he was holding onto one of the cots and said, "Drape them things around your limbs, gents."

"I thought you was gonna help us bust out of here," protested Wade McKitrick.

"Just do it," Rain said angrily.

"You hear that?" questioned Canada Reese. "Sounds like that lynch mob is on the way."

Hurriedly the gunhands put on the irons, and then to hobble behind Canada bringing them into the office and to the back room, where Rain covered their prisoners while Canada removed four long guns from a gun rack and found matching lead slugs in boxes. Then he was outside and going ahead again toward their stolen wagon. Rain opened the back door of the marshal's wagon, with his gesturing gun bringing the McKitricks inside. He closed and locked the door, hurried around to find Canada stowing the weapons he'd taken in a storage box under the high front seat. Clambering up, it was to have Canada unfasten the reins and gee the horses to the left and away from the back of the jail. Rain twisted around where he sat next to Canada, and just before they swung southward and passed behind a building, he spotted several men moving into the alleyway and entering the jail.

"Pick it up a little," he told Canada.

"Nervous?"

"Considering we're perched on property stolen from the U.S. government, got stolen hosses hitched to it, and we are jailbreakers, yup."

Coming to one of the main thoroughfares, Canada wheeled to his left and urged the horses into a fast lope. It wasn't until the last building fell behind and the eastward road began curling upward that a tug on the reins brought the horses to a walk, and with him uttering, "This marshal's wagon pulls mighty fine."

"Just so these horses don't wear out."

"If the going gets tough, Rain, we could leave the wagon and ride them hosses."

"I find it kind of comforting having the McKitricks shackled hand and foot and behind bars of a fashion. This'll have to do until we clear Bozeman Pass and get to Livingston."

Canada Reese, remembering how the passenger train they were on had to labor through the pass, said, "There's some rough spots on that stagecoach road . . . but us getting through hinges on how

192

long it'll be before that sheriff figures this out and comes after us."

This brought Rain Lonigan's eyes probing the mountain range to either side as the road began edging into the pass. There was enough moonlight beaming onto the approaches for both men and horses to keep to the road, while above the pine forest of the mountain patches of snow lay along the peaks. They had stowed their saddles on the roof of the wagon, and their warbags, and now the increasing chill as they climbed higher brought Rain crawling back and finding his sheepskin and Canada's old mackinaw.

"While you're back there, pass up that bottle of whiskey I cached."

Rain found the bottle, slipped back onto the seat where he donned his coat, and afterward to take the reins from Canada. Over the steady clop-clop of the horses moving at an upward angle came the nearby rustling of a creek. Close at hand the pine trees stood motionless, mute witnesses to the passage of their marshal's wagon.

"I'm trying not to think of how far we've got to go."

"Or how far we've come," countered the plainsman. "What's that old adage, that possession is nine-tenths of the law."

"See those trees," said Rain, "there's a lot of tempting branches just high enough for a hanging. But we do that . . . I reckon we're no better'n Modahl and those others." The bottle was passed to him, and he drank sparingly.

"Suppose you're right."

193

"Yup, it's only fitting our neighbors back at Squaw Gap get to sit in judgment over these killers."

Chapter Nineteen

"What do you mean they're gone?"

Ella Farnsworth stood just outside her bedroom door clothed in a velvety black gown, one hand clutching a derringer in concealment at her side. Upon hearing Frank Modahl's horse come pounding up, she'd taken the weapon out of a dresser drawer, and until this frightening moment she had had every intention of using it to kill Modahl. But now she had trouble breathing, so great was her fear because the McKitricks had gotten away.

"Somebody came in first and busted them out is all I know."

"Springer is pulling a doublecross!"

"Like hell Springer is, Ella. When I left Springer he was forming a posse. The sheriff figures it was this hombre from the Dakotas busting the McKitricks out of jail. He came in this afternoon wanting Sheriff Springer to hand them over so's he could take them back to stand trial. A hombre name of Lonigan; marshal back there at Squaw Gap."

"I don't give a damn about this marshal, Frank. I want them dead . . . do you understand!"

"Simmer down, dammit," he muttered sourly.

"A thousand to have them killed."

"A thousand apiece or you can go after them yourself."

"Just do it then."

"A deal, honeysuckle. The boys are waiting over by the jail. Springer has it laid out that some head out on horseback, the rest by train. That we'll catch up to them in Bozeman Pass."

"And, Frank, no excuses this time."

"Yeah, yeah," he muttered as he turned to go up the hallway, "you'd better get your beauty rest, honeysuckle, as you sure in hell look awful haggard."

Frank Modahl hurried out to his bronc, and saddlebound, loped it back to men milling about in front of the jail. Just upstreet others had crowded into a saloon, and every so often someone would come out and look to see if the posse being gathered by Sheriff Springer was ready to move out. Modahl tied up across the street, to be promptly joined by two other hardcases.

"It's going onto four o'clock, Frank. In a couple of hours a passenger train is due in from Butte."

"We'll be on it."

"The sheriff has told the depot agent he wants two or three cattle cars hooked up to the train."

"Head over to the saloon," Modahl told them, and as those he rode the outlaw trail with moved away, Modahl picked his way through the press and went into Sheriff Toby Springer's office.

Springer asked quietly, "You talked to Ella?"

"She wants 'em dead."

"Figures. I suppose you're coming along?"

Frank Modahl grinned. "The way you got this

196

figured out, Toby, us taking after them on that train, once we catch them up in Bozeman Pass it'll be a turkey shoot."

"That damned Lonigan stole some of my guns."

"Won't make any difference when you consider around fifty men will be on that train."

"Yeah," muttered the sheriff, "I'd sure hate to be Lonigan."

"Or them murdering McKitricks."

This was the second time since midnight that one of T. Hartwig's deputy U.S. marshals had come up the back staircase, the tramping of the man's boots sounding hellishly loud through the open bedroom window. The springs on the brass bed creaked when Hartwig swung his legs to the floor and shoved to a sitting position. Even through the faded longjohns he could feel the chill of night, and Hartwig knew he should have closed the windows in his room on the second floor of Anne Brannigan's boarding house. But long nights on the trail had gotten him used to frosty night air. He hawked spleen into his mouth as the deputy rapped urgently on the door frame.

"Come," he said hoarsely. Rising, the braces on his trousers brushing against the back of his knees, U.S. Marshal T. Hartwig swept the curtain aside and spat out a window. He was in an owly mood, and glad that his scowl didn't show in the dark room as he swung around. "Spit it out, Ramsey."

"It was like you figured, sir, that lawman from

Squaw Gap breaking out the McKitricks. The sheriff is really pissed off about it."

"Me too, if the truth be known."

"Ah . . . the sheriff is fixing to take after them on a passenger train due within the hour."

"Sounds like Springer."

"Right now they're loading their horses into cattle cars. And . . . and, sir, there's something else . . ."

Hartwig slumped onto a chair and reached for his boots.

"That new marshal's wagon has been stolen."

"Stolen?" he said crossly.

"Someone saw that wagon pulling out of town around the time the McKitricks were busted out."

"Lonigan," he murmured with a rueful shake of his head. "My fault." He came erect, to put on a gray woolen shirt, and buttoning it, he added, "Is everything set?"

"Yup . . . yessir, Marshal Hartwig. Shelby and Mortenson are waiting with the horses."

"Go ease their minds; I'll be down shortly."

Alone, he turned to a small table and lit the lamp perched on it, and also his gunbelt and dark brown Stetson. He was careful about strapping the gunbelt around his waist as he pondered over the night's happenings. His informants around Bozeman had told him about Sheriff Springer's occasional visits to see the Widow Farnsworth. He knew she'd hired this hardcase, Frank Modahl, and others. So it came as no surprise to Marshal T. Hartwig the news about Wade McKitrick escaping from that railroad work gang. He also knew

198

of the widow Farnsworth's entanglement with Johnston Pettigrew; hell, everyone knew about that from here to Butte. But what T. Hartwig hadn't figured out was how she had gotten the McKitricks to do that killing job over at Squaw Gap. The plain fact was the McKitricks blamed the widow Farnsworth and her departed husband, and of course, Pettigrew, for getting chased out of Bozeman. Another puzzle to him was the sheriff getting mixed up in this. Most of this had been cleared up with the unexpected return of Tanner and Wade McKitrick, and Blaine.

"Come back to collect their blood money is how I see it." His left hand dropping away from his Stetson squared atop his balding head, he brought it to a leather coat hanging amongst others in a small closet, with his right hand plucking a couple of boxes of .44-40 caliber cartridges, these for his sixgun and the chambered Winchester '73, his reliable center-fire repeating rifle. Reaching for the Winchester snugged up on a hand-carved rifle rack, he bent to blow out the lamp, and hawked up more sputum as he let the screen door bang behind him. A chain-smoker, this of handrolled cigars, he was seldom without a raspy feeling in his throat, but T. Hartwig figured savoring those cigars was worth the price.

The staircase creaking as he clambered down, the U.S. marshal nodded brusquely to the trio of deputy marshals. "A hell of a way to start any day." Shoving the Winchester into the scabbard, he swung aboard the big gelding. He cleared his throat, but instead of saying anything, he pulled out a cigar from an ample supply in his coat pocket and bit one end away before wedging it between his teeth. The tradition of lighting it over, as well as that first savory inhaling of smoke, he laid squinting eyes upon those with him.

"That train scheduled to pull out at six?"

"Yessir."

"Will be delayed some coupling up those extra cars. So, what it'll be is us lawmen taking out after another, this Lonigan from Squaw Gap. I only hope we get there before Sheriff Springer and that mob."

"You fixing on arresting Lonigan for stealing that marshal's wagon?"

"Don't rightly know. Most likely we'll have to bury Lonigan and the McKitricks out there if we don't get a move on."

Then U.S. Marshal T. Hartwig spurred around the rooming house, inhaling cigar smoke, and setting his thoughts on the nearby peaks and the high gap between which would carry him up into Bozeman Pass.

About five miles into Bozeman Pass the engineer of Northern Pacific engine #53 pushed the throttle-lever forward, causing the train to grind slowly to a halt on an upgrade. Behind him in the cab stood one of Sheriff Springer's deputies, who'd leaned out and was looking back along the passenger cars at members of the posse bringing their saddled horses out of a cattle car.

The passenger train was hugging a serrated

200

mountain wall rising a few hundred feet to still more mountain, forming a rocky crest. They were on the north wall of the pass. Portions of the stagecoach road could be seen near the floor of the deep pass, and a mountain stream glinting whenever the sun cleared patches of cloud. Covering the rugged terrain of Bozeman Pass and stippling up the slopes were thick stands of limber pine and Douglas fir.

"Move out," the deputy ordered.

"How many of you got on my train?"

"Dunno, forty, fifty."

As engine #53 strained up the angling track, the engineer said, "Fifty of you against one man. Maybe your sheriff should have wired ahead to have cavalrymen sent out from Fort Ellis."

Deputy Sheriff Ray Faraday had to smile at the engineer's derisive comment, and Faraday drawled, "The sheriff is really worked up about the McKitricks getting away. It sure is kind of funny how he knew the McKitricks were coming in before . . . almost as if . . ."

Faraday left it there as he peeled his eyes out of the jostling cab of the engine to gaze at fifteen men who'd been on this train urging their mounts down toward the ribbon of stagecoach road. When he'd been taken on as a deputy by Sheriff Springer there hadn't been all this trouble with the McKitricks and Lydel Farnsworth. Springer, in his opinion, had his sour moments, and was hard to work for, but he considered the sheriff to have an honest character. Somehow, though he couldn't prove it, Sheriff Springer had gotten mixed up with

Johnston Pettigrew, a known associate at the time of Tanner and Wade McKitrick, and after this thing had busted open, with both Pettigrew and the McKitricks pulling out, Springer had gotten involved with Farnsworth's widow, Ella. And now there was Frank Modahl. Back at the jail he'd overheard Modahl telling the sheriff that the McKitricks and Marshal Lonigan had to be gunned down, with Sheriff Springer agreeing. He could see this being done to Tanner and Wade McKitrick, but murdering another law officer didn't sound right to Deputy Sheriff Ray Faraday.

He let his gaze drift eastward to the pass wending through the high peaks, Mt. Blackmore dominating to the south, opposite the Bridgers. He knew Bozeman Pass to be around twenty-five miles of rugged terrain, that any kind of vehicle passing through it did so at considerable risk. A glance sunward told Faraday it was going on mid-afternoon. And that by rights he should stick to this train when that marshal's wagon was sighted and not get off until he was as far east as Miles City or maybe beyond.

"This is just out-and-out murder."

Conductor Alex Grissom wasn't all that happy at the way these men had stormed aboard his train back at Bozeman, men armed with rifles and full of bold talk, to scare passengers out of that back car. Farther up the line he had every intention of writing out a report of this infraction and forwarding it on to the division manager. This report

202

would include the delay caused by those cattle cars being hooked onto the train. He'd been in that passenger car when the sheriff of Gallatin County had told Grissom to stop the train in order to let off some of his men.

In the conductor's opinion most of these weren't law abiding citizens but a scattering of ruffians and hardcases, their talk of how they meant to wipe out those who'd escaped from jail. In a way Conductor Grissom had to agree with their bragging talk, since the escapees in question were the McKitrick brothers.

"Sheriff, we're way behind schedule."

"Can't be helped," replied Toby Springer. "We're about halfway through the pass. Should be spotting that stolen wagon most any time. Then we'll get our horses and this train can make up for lost time."

"A testy sonofabitch," muttered Frank Modahl as the conductor went back up the aisle and left the passenger car. He laid a thoughtful fist down on the window sill and added, "Should be some readers out on the McKitricks."

"Maybe too damned many."

"I expect most of them will read dead or alive. Would be nice collecting some of the reward money . . . unless, Sheriff, you figure on hogging all of it."

"First we have to find them."

"You didn't answer my question."

"A split then . . . but just between us," he said grudgingly.

Removing his hat to show the red ring around

his upper forehead, Modahl ran his hand around the inner lining to wipe away a little tracing of sweat as he said, "If it hadn't been for Ella Farnsworth, I would have killed that Wade McKitrick down in Wyoming. Got a real mean mouth. This Lonigan, I suppose he's got Wade and Tanner all hogtied in them irons he stole and locked up in that wagon. So all we're facing is one gun."

"You talk like you're worried—"

"Worry, Springer, is what keeps me alive. A man don't fret none about things he don't last long out here. Worry—you bet, about catching them . . . and about sharing any reward money with you. Yup, Sheriff, I'm a bundle of worry."

Chapter Twenty

"What do you think?"

"That wheel won't last much longer."

"We're still climbing."

"Never seems any end to this pass."

"Dammit," groused Tanner McKitrick through a barred window in the marshal's wagon, "at least we can get out to get some of that creek water."

"None of us have eaten since yesterday," Rain Lonigan said to the plainsman. "Be as good a place as any to chow down."

"There ain't much," said Canada, "just some prairie strawberries and maybe enough beef jerky for one meal. Or I could pick off one of those squirrels." He nodded upward at Douglas firs bunched to either side of the creek.

"That'll mean building a fire," Rain said worriedly. "Open those cans of beans while I tend to our prisoners."

"You want help watching them?"

"It would be tempting gunning them down if they try anything," he said loudly for the benefit of the McKitricks. He stepped around behind the marshal's wagon hogging the middle of the stagecoach road whereas the horses were angled off it and the front pair held there by lead ropes looped around low branches. Unlocking the door, he swung it open and motioned for those inside to come out.

"A long, bumpy ride," commented Tanner McKitrick as he jumped down to the gravelly track and slipped a little before regaining his balance and composure. Next came Wade with a sneer for Rain Lonigan, and with the bitter resentment of being in irons etched on his stubbled face.

"A long, bumpy ride for all of us," said Rain. He made no attempt to unlimber his sixgun but simply nodded toward the nearby creek.

"So you figure you saved us from a lynch mob?" jeered Wade McKitrick.

Ever since breaking out, the McKitricks, and in the hours before when he and Canada had been forced to steal property belonging to others, Rain had been walking a tension-packed line. And all he could think of now was how these men had killed his wife. He grabbed Wade McKitrick's shoulder, spun the man around, brought his clenched fist slamming at Wade's face. The outlaw stumbled backward, with Rain hitting McKitrick again to have him topple into the shallow creek waters.

"Easy, Rain, easy," chided Canada Reese, who kept a watchful eye on the other McKitrick.

Wading out, Rain yelled, "Drink all the creek water you want, McKitrick. You'd be dead by now if we hadn't been damned fools and broke you out of jail. Damn you."

"I apologize for my brother," said Tanner McKitrick as he closed in on the creek and sprawled down on the bank, to drink thirstily. When he'd sated his thirst, he came awkwardly to his knees. "You broke us out, Lonigan, just to take us back to stand trial. What's to keep you and your partner from finishing us off out here?"

"Because," broke in Canada, "Rain Lonigan ain't a lowlife like you or your mangy brother. You hear that?" He looked quizzically to the west.

"A train," Rain said after a few moments. "Probably heave into sight any minute now."

Canada shuffled over and handed Tanner McKitrick an opened can of beans and some beef jerky, to have Tanner say, "No fork to get at them?"

"Use your fingers, damn it."

Picking up some jerky, Rain began chewing on it as he went over to a pine and sat down with his back against it. He removed his left boot and dumped the water out as a Northern Pacific passenger train rounded a distant bend in the pass. Striking out at Wade McKitrick had released some of his anger, but there was no remorse in Rain for having hit a man shackled as Wade was, for the outlaw would do the same to him or worse under the same circumstances.

Canada Reese, coming over but angling so he could watch their prisoners, nodded at the passenger train back a ways but higher on the sheer wall of the pass. "It could be by now, Rain, that sheriff has figured out it was you breaking out Tanner and Wade. Could be on that train."

"We're out in the open; so's our wagon."

"Or maybe not."

"I get this feeling Sheriff Springer is closing in

207

on us. He could have dropped some men off behind us with hosses they've brought along. Then all they'd have to do is stop the train someplace ahead and box us in."

"That being the case, we'd best get a move on. Come on, you ornery cusses, back into your cage."

Tanner McKitrick, as he moved reluctantly toward the narrow road and their wagon, said, "I couldn't help overhearing what you just said. If the sheriff pulled his deputies away from that jail in Bozeman, it means he's working with Farnsworth's wife. Dead we can't testify against her or the sheriff. Knowing Springer, he'll have plenty of men with him."

"There's no way I'm arming you or your brother."

"You might have to, Lonigan. For the way I see it, the sheriff can't afford to leave any witnesses behind."

"Into the wagon, McKitrick. Come on, move it . . . and you, Wade." Grimly he watched them struggle up into the wagon, to afterward close and lock the door. Coming around the marshal's wagon, he took a look at the right front wheel, realized they'd have to set a slower pace. And realizing also that it was just possible that the wagon had been spotted as that train was almost opposite them in the pass. He clambered up beside Canada, to have Canada Reese bring the wagon upward on the weathered trail.

"Now I'm glad you had sense enough to fetch along some spare weapons."

"Never can have enough of them at times like this. But maybe that sheriff isn't on that train. That maybe Springer wired ahead to Livingston to have the law there handle this."

"After what Tanner McKitrick just told us, Sheriff Springer's almost certain to be on that train. I don't see it slacking down any."

Canada grimaced when the wagon lurched because of that busted wheel, but he kept the horses to a lope on a fairly level reach of road, and with both of them suddenly realizing they weren't climbing as much. About fifteen minutes later a nudge from Canada brought Rain's eyes lifting to sunlight glinting off something farther eastward along the pass.

"Could be another wagon coming through or—"

"Or some riders."

"A bunch of them for damned certain," said Canada as a pair of horsemen loped into view perhaps two or three miles in the direction they were going, now others in a long ragged column.

"Canada, now I'm sorry I got you into this."

"Haven't had this much fun in a long time. Been outnumbered before, so's these hombres won't be going against no greenhorn. There's a likely spot to stand them off; bunch of boulders along the creek."

"Head in there. It'll be better than having them catch us out in the open."

"Get down there," yelled Canada to the horses, and to have him rein them off the road and go down an abrupt hunk of land and then wedge the wagon under sheltering firs.

While Canada clambered down to tend to the horses, Rain dug the spare guns out of the storage box along with boxes of shells. He brought these down into the jumbled mess of boulders forming a natural barrier through which the creek flowed. Briefly he considered leaving their prisoners in the wagon, but realized the wagon would be an irresistible target for the sheriff and his mob. Returning to the wagon, he let out the McKitricks.

"We've got company. So just head in amongst these rocks."

"How many?"

"Enough to make a man work up a sweat."

"Lonigan, I'd sure hate to go down under their guns without being given a chance to return their fire."

"Move it, bogus preacher."

"Rain," called out Canada, "here those buzzards come." Then the plainsman scrambled after Rain and the outlaws, finding a narrow gap between two boulders. When he got in there, Canada picked up one of the stolen rifles and began arming it with lead slugs.

While Rain Lonigan murmured silently, "Maybe I've overplayed my hand." With his sixgun in hand, he watched the riders come to an uncertain halt farther east on the stagecoach road. He recognized the sheriff on his rangy sorrel, Springer arguing with another rider. And now when the horsemen spread out and began pulling out long guns or revolvers he no longer had any doubts about what was to happen.

* * *

"They should be around here someplace," questioned Sheriff Toby Springer. "Since we haven't seen any fresh wagon tracks coming this far."

"Well, Springer," Frank Modahl said chidingly, "about the only way they can get up these canyon walls is if they suddenly sprout wings. I figure they're holed up down along the creek someplace."

"Could be they're still coming this way on the road," said one of the deputies.

"That train made one helluva racket cutting through here. If Lonigan has any smarts at all, he'll know we were on it."

"You're probably right," said Sheriff Springer. He reined his horse sideways in the narrow confines of the road to face those he'd brought along. The first bunch of men who'd been dropped off, this back to the west about six or seven miles, had been culled out as being too unreliable in the sheriff's opinion, meaning they were the lawabiding element of Bozeman. Those he stared at now were Frank Modahl and his hardcase associates, the rest just drifters or men he knew who would have no qualms about wiping out that meddling lawman from Squaw Gap and the McKitricks. At the moment he felt damned good about how things were shaping up, and he crafted a smile.

Whereupon Springer said, "You men spread out north to the creek and beyond to the north wall. Then we'll sweep to the west. As I said before, Lonigan's vowed not to be taken alive. So if you spot anything, commence firing." The sharp clicking of Springer working the lever on his Winchester was the signal that brought the riders into motion. That same smile held as he let his horse prance nervously up the stagecoach road.

About an hour and a half ago U.S. Marshal T. Hartwig had heard that Northern Pacific passenger car laboring eastward, but at the time the marshal and his deputies had been passing through a thick stand of firs. Coming out, though, they'd seen the black smoke belching back over the hind end of the train just before it plunged around a bend in the canyon wall.

His comment had been terse and to the point, "Either we pick up the pace some or Lonigan is as good as six feet under. Or knowing our honorable sheriff, he'll leave the bodies for the turkey vultures."

After track had been laid through Bozeman Pass, to have freight and passenger trains come through on a regular basis, the stagecoach companies had been forced out of business. As a result, the road followed by Marshal T. Hartwig wasn't kept up as in the old days. Washouts were commonplace, with small rivulets cutting across the seldom-used road. While the iron rims of the stolen marshal's wagon had left indentations to marks its passage through here.

Deputy Marshal Mortenson, having pressed ahead of the others, suddenly called back, "Fresh tracks up here, Marshal Hartwig." When the others came up, he added, "I count at least fourteen riders."

Hartwig could see fresh hoof markings coming onto the road from the north. "Part of that so-called posse. They shouldn't be that far ahead of us."

Pressing on, the sun more at their backs, the federal lawmen finally had to bring their tiring horses down toward the creek bank. A brief halt in which they refilled their canteens and let the horses drink sparingly. In the saddle again, Hartwig urged his horse into a canter. Another mile of hard riding gave the lawmen their first glimpse of riders on a distant and higher elevation. Without hesitating the marshal unleathered his sidearm and fired upward. At first a few of the riders ahead just twisted in the saddle to look back, with Hartwig's gun sounding once more to halt all of those chasing after Rain Lonigan. It took the lawmen about fifteen minutes to come up to the posse.

"I thought I recognized you, Marshal Hartwig."

"Milner, you boys know why you're here?"

"To catch those murdering McKitricks."

"I expect it is chiefly to help Sheriff Springer murder another lawman."

"Why, we were told that friends of the McKitricks busted them out of jail."

"Another lawman did that; the marshal of Squaw Gap. And not to help them escape justice, Milner, but to keep them from being lynched. So, boys, how's it gonna be?"

"We've been deputized, Marshal Hartwig."

"Yup, and we aim to catch those outlaws."

"You'll do so only if you boys obey my orders.

Riding with the sheriff is a man named Frank Modahl. I'll explain most of this later. But Modahl, and Sheriff Springer, mean to leave no survivors. Meaning that when we get there . . . we're gonna try to keep Marshal Lonigan and the McKitricks alive."

"That'll mean going against the sheriff."

"It'll mean my not having to arrest you boys later for aiding and abetting murder. Now let's shag the hell out of here."

Chapter Twenty-one

"Bammity — Bam-Bam-Bam!"

Why was it in this thin mountain air a bullet seemed to travel a lot faster, but a man had trouble dragging the same air into his heaving lungs. Rain and Canada Reese and the McKitricks huddled a little lower among the sheltering rocks could feel the sting of bits of rock chipped away by leaden slugs seeking flesh. Though Canada, when he'd picked out this cul-de-sac of boulders, had noticed there were very few trees close at hand, that if the posse began closing in, they'd do so with just those few trees and maybe another boulder or two to give them cover. While the horses tethered to the marshal's wagon were bucking and threatening to bust out of their traces.

"I expect," said Canada, "they'll go for our hosses."

"I expect so," said Rain through clenched teeth as a bullet slammed into a sheltering boulder and went rattling among other hunks of rock before whining away. "How many are there?"

"Maybe a couple of hundred?" Canada Reese chuckled at what he'd just uttered, and then sighting in on a black hat tipping up above a boulder, he pulled the trigger on his rifle. There was a startled yelp as the hat danced away. "But enough of them, Rain."

"Lonigan, you got no right to keep us chained like this."

"Well, I'll tell you what you can do," he said back to Wade McKitrick, "you can heave your butt up and introduce yourself to our unwelcome guests."

"Damn you, Lonigan."

Then Rain blinked in pain when a shard of rock slapped at his neck. The hand he brought up came away tinted with blood. Worming onto his right side, lifting the rifle to his left cheek, he spotted a man wearing a checkered shirt just breaking in closer, and though he was aiming from an unnatural off-hand position, when his rifle barked the slug flaming out of its barrel punched into checkered shirt's abdomen. He didn't watch the man crumble groundward but swiveled the barrel while pumping the lever. This time when he fired his rifle it was to shatter the leg of a man scrambling back to cover. But for Rain Lonigan there was little satisfaction in trying to kill these men, for he knew they'd been brought out here by order of Sheriff Toby Springer. And maybe, he mused hopefully, if we take out a few more they'll pull back. But that hope was shattered by one of their horses letting out an agonizing neigh.

Canada Reese's bitter shout of protest resounded over the steady tattoo of lead slugs, "No man worth his salt would gun down a horse."

Rolling over and deeper into the recesses of the rocks, Rain worked his way among them until he could view the marshal's wagon, rocking as the horses hitched to it seemed to break every which way, the one horse just hit struggling on its side in its tethering pieces of leather, its mate breaking away from the stench of blood and death, the back horses trying to break ahead. Now they watched as the other horses were hit, one simply dropping over dead, the two still alive buckling and whickering in fear and pain.

"Wade's breaking away!" warned Canada Reese.

Twisting around, Rain glimpsed the outlaw plunging into the creek with one of their rifles, and the other one, Tanner McKitrick, trying to fumble a bullet into another rifle.

"Let it be!" yelled Rain.

"No, they're gonna kill all of us!"

"I said leave it be!" The bullet fired from Rain's long gun slapped into the stock of the rifle to have it knocked away from McKitrick.

The next moment all of them became aware of Wade McKitrick's cry for help, and when their eyes finally located the outlaw, so had the concentrated gunfire from their attackers. He still managed to clutch the rifle in his weakening grasp, still stood upward in the creek, blood staining his left cheekbone and more along his scalpline, his midriff and chest showing where he'd just been hit. Just before Wade McKitrick began toppling over, another lead slug came by to penetrate his right eye socket, the slug exiting through the back of his head. Then he was slipping under the watery surface.

"Damn," swore Tanner McKitrick, "they tore him apart."

With the death of Wade McKitrick the gunfire tapered off, though a few bullets slapped in to remind those encircled in that jumble of rocks they were still under siege. It suddenly dawned on Rain that in about an hour the sun would strike back over those western mountains. He took the time now to reload his rifle as he asked, "You okay, Canada?"

"Got nicked a little," he shrugged.

"McKitrick?"

"Still wanting to get these irons removed. Once it gets dark they'll come in. From the way they opened fire, Lonigan, it seems the sheriff isn't gonna take any prisoners."

"So Springer was in on this."

"What Springer hasn't taken into account is that he might take us out. But as sure as a full house beats two pair, the widow Farnsworth will have Modahl polish off the sheriff. I'm figuring after that she'll do the same to Frank Modahl. Why not give me a halfway decent chance at making a break for it. I don't need no weapon; just unshackle these irons and I'll try to get away."

"I didn't come all this way just to catch you and then let you go, McKitrick."

"Lonigan!"

"Someone beckons, Rain."

Rain stole a look around a boulder, where he could see Frank Modahl standing in long shadows cast by a Douglas fir, and with Modahl shouting again, "You give it up, Lonigan, and you can walk out of here. All we want is Tanner McKitrick."

He glanced over at the outlaw, and Rain said,

"What do you say, Tanner?"

"You're calling the shots."

"You like the hat he's wearing, Canada?"

"Something of an eyesore." The plainsman peered down the long barrel of his rifle, then he unleashed a bullet that spun Modahl's hat away, and with the hardcase lunging behind the tree.

Now the guns of the posse cut loose with a deadly and deafening salvo, but this time under the urging of the sheriff and a yelling Frank Modahl they began coming in for the kill.

"Maybe I should have aimed a little lower . . ."

"Too late to worry about that now," said Rain as he went into a crouch and fanned out bullets at the onslaughters until the hammer clicked shut on an empty chamber.

But now, with the sun edging behind the distant peaks, some of those who'd slipped around to come in from the west and along brush shielding the creek, suddenly became aware of horsemen pounding in, that four of the newcomers wore U.S. marshal's stars. And at dusking there was still enough light for them to make out the lawmen were members of the posse.

"You men," shouted Marshal T. Hartwig, "cease fire!"

"Not when we've got the McKitricks holed up like this."

Suddenly in the hand of U.S. Marshal Hartwig was his sixgun, and he barked out, "Do it or I'll drop you where you stand, mister. Shelby, Mortenson, head up yonder and let those men see your badges. What about the sheriff, is he on this side?"

"Coming in beyond that wagon."

"I expect Modahl is with the sheriff?"

"Last I seen of Modahl he was."

Slowly the firing died out, though it still came from the east, and once in a while from the stones ringing the marshal from Squaw Gap. At a word from Hartwig his deputies and the other newcomers swung down, but the marshal kept to the saddle as he spurred his bronc up along the stagecoach road.

"Lonigan, you hear me?"

Rain snaked a look in the direction of the road.

"I expect you recall coming to my office at the courthouse," yelled Hartwig.

"Yeah, Hartwig, and damned glad you're here." Rain ducked as a bullet crawled along his sideburn and struck rock behind him. "But you'd better announce yourself to the sheriff."

To the east and just slipping in behind another tree that brought him closer to the men he was trying to kill, Sheriff Toby Springer glanced over at Frank Modahl, and Springer said, "Damn the luck; Hartwig's here."

"To hell with him," said Modahl. "You men, keep firing them weapons. Then you, you, and you, break in there." And as Modahl fired again, so did the sheriff, to give covering fire for those darting out into the open.

While up on the road Marshal Hartwig spurred down off the road and managed to wound two of those moving in toward the bouldery refuge. Coming under the trees, he swung down just as Springer opened up at him, but the return fire from the U.S. marshal punched a couple of holes in the sheriff's chest.

"Modahl . . . look . . . out . . ."

Frank Modahl swung that way in time to see Springer crumble onto pine needles strewing the ground under the trees. The hardcase snapped off a shot that struck a branch, and a desperate glint coming into his eyes, he broke to the east. He made it to his horse and was swinging a leg over the back of his horse only to have Hartwig cry out as he appeared, "Don't make me do it, Modahl! Chuck that sixgun and get off that bronc!"

The hardcase hesitated, not wanting to be gunned down by the marshal, but gripped with an arrogant fury that made him hold onto his weapon. Then the marshal's weapon barked to have a bullet slap into Frank Modahl's gunhand.

"Go on," taunted U.S. Marshal T. Hartwig, "you've still got one good hand . . . so go for your rifle."

"No, damn you," he muttered as he crawled down from the saddle.

Grabbing Modahl's shoulder, the marshal pushed the man into a shambling walk that brought them back through the trees and to the opening beyond which lay the boulders. Hartwig said angrily, "Tell everyone to cease fire, Modahl, or this time I'll blow one of your kneecaps away. Do it, man!"

Clutching at his wounded hand, Frank Modahl shouted, "It's over . . . cease fire . . . dammit!"

Chapter Twenty-two

Once again Rain Lonigan found himself on a train, but eastbound this time. Only it was without Tanner McKitrick as a prisoner, but with the plainsman, Canada Reese, seated facing him. At the moment they were beyond Miles City, with the expectation of viewing the Badlands before nooning.

Despite his having testified against Ella Farnsworth, the outlaw Tanner McKitrick had been sentenced to die by hanging. The trial at Bozeman hadn't taken all that long, but for Rain Lonigan it had been a time to reflect on what his future held. Mostly it was that he didn't want to keep on with ranching, especially at a place that held so many memories.

"You're sorrowful company, Rain."

"I'm sorry, I . . ."

"You're still carrying all of this hatred. All it will do, Rain, is tarnish the memory of your wife."

"Canada . . . it's . . . it's more like an empty void in me."

The plainsman reached over and placed a comforting hand on Rain's arm, and to have him say gently, "What you've got, Rain, is a wounded heart. Only time will heal how you feel. At least you've got more than me back there . . ."

"Yes . . . my children." A sparkle came into Rain Lonigan's eyes.

"Lordy," said Canada as he craned his head for a sidelong look out through the open window, "I do believe we're coming onto the Badlands."

"Yes, home—home where the heart is."